VOLUME THREE

A Cup of
CHRISTMAS CHEER

HEARTWARMING TALES *of*
CHRISTMAS PAST

Guideposts
New York

A Cup of Christmas Cheer is a trademark of Guideposts.

Published by Guideposts Books & Inspirational Media
110 William Street
New York, NY 10038
Guideposts.org

Acknowledgments

Every attempt has been made to credit the sources of copyrighted material used in this book. If any such acknowledgment has been inadvertently omitted or miscredited, receipt of such information would be appreciated.

Cover and interior design by Müllerhaus
Illustrated by Greg Copeland, represented by Deborah Wolfe, LTD
Typeset by Aptara

Printed and bound in the United States of America
10 9 8 7 6 5 4 3 2 1

Contents

THE CHRISTMAS SCARF

Liz Johnson

Philadelphia, December 1975

Katherine Sullivan had been carrying around a bright red scarf with tassels on the ends since she was twelve years old. She'd been searching for its rightful owner for almost as long.

"Kate, what are you staring at?"

She spun around at the gentle hand on her shoulder, turning from the two men in green military fatigues who strolled along the far sidewalk.

Janie Walsh, a tall woman with black hair escaping her white nurse's cap, wore a frown of confusion. "We've got to get inside or we'll be late for our shift."

A bitter wind whipped past the seven-story hospital, catching traces of snow and soot and twirling them between rusted cars and shivering pedestrians. A chill raced up Kate's legs, and she tugged at the lapels of her jacket and rubbed her hands together.

"They might know him," she whispered. A bubble of hope swelled in her chest as the two men crossed three lanes of traffic and turned toward the YMCA. From this distance, she couldn't make out the words on the sleeves of their jackets, but she'd recognize the eagle, globe, and anchor of the Marine Corps insignia from any distance. They too were back from Vietnam. And maybe, just maybe, they had seen her brother.

Janie's frown deepened. "You can't just run up to every man back from the war and shove a picture in his face."

"Says who?" Before the words were even out, Kate launched into the street, checking for traffic as she tried to dodge patches of ice. The wind licked at her cap, and she clapped a hand on top of it. The head nurse wouldn't let her start her shift if she was out of uniform. Or late.

Picking up her pace and shifting the green bag on her shoulder, Kate called out as the men turned the corner into a narrow alley. "Excuse me! Please! May I ask you a question?"

Either they didn't hear her or they chose not to, disappearing into the glare of the late-afternoon sun. Kate scurried around the corner just as a gust of wind kicked up the smoke coming from a barrel fire halfway down the alley.

"Please," she called again.

A hand touched her shoulder, and she jerked away until she caught sight of Janie's raven curls and timid smile.

Kate mouthed a thank-you to her friend, who didn't have to follow. And one look at the three skinny figures hovering near the fire's heat was more than enough to make her thankful she wasn't alone in this alley. All three men smirked at her from beneath puffy, weary eyes, and her stomach jolted.

Digging into her bag, Kate pulled out a long blue scarf and another in orange before plastering what she hoped was a confident smile into place.

"Would you like a scarf?" She held them at arm's length, Janie's warmth at her side giving her an extra dose of confidence.

The man in the middle was shorter than the others, the brown facial hair around his mouth a little more noticeable. Nodding his chin in her direction, he asked, "You make those?"

"Yes." Kate shuffled forward, reaching out even further. Janie's breathing picked up speed, but she didn't leave Kate's side. "I have enough for each of you."

"What do you want for it?" This from the man in camouflage pants. His face, while hard, was still young.

He couldn't be much older than Stephen. Maybe not even twenty-five. But the homeless life, the addicted life, left a telltale mark.

She blinked, her arm falling to her side and her shoulders sagging. "Nothing."

The rail-thin kid on the end scowled. "Nothing's for nothing."

"Please." The word came out as a croak, and she cleared her throat. "My brother is a marine. I…I was hoping you might have seen him—might know where he is."

Three matching frowns filled the silence, and Janie tugged on her arm. "Let's go."

Then—from somewhere beyond the barrel—a deep voice rose above the crackle of burning newsprint. "You got a picture of him?"

Kate nearly dropped her scarves and bag, tripping over herself to produce the two-inch image of Stephen Matthews. He was all things handsome and charming in his crisp service uniform, his garrison cap tilting ever-so-slightly toward his right eye, which was as blue as Kate knew her own to be. His red hair wasn't quite as vibrant as hers, but no one had ever missed their family connection.

"Yes! Of course!" She ran forward, her arm extended with the photograph Stephen had sent in his first—his only—letter.

Taking their cues from the man who had remained hidden until then, the original trio hunched over the picture, squinting hard. Eventually they all shook their heads. "Never seen him before."

"Nope."

Tears pricked at the back of her eyes, and Kate blinked. Of course they didn't know Stephen. Philadelphia was an enormous city, and she couldn't even be certain he'd returned to their hometown after his time in Vietnam. Not after the stand their father had taken.

"Come on, Kate." Janie tugged on her arm. "We have to go or we'll be late for our shift."

"Just a minute." She turned back to the men, gifting each with a knitted scarf and a smile. "Thank you."

"For what?"

"For coming home."

THREE DAYS LATER, KATE STEPPED INTO THE CAFETERIA OF St. Jude's Mission. Someone had set up three towering pine trees in the far corners since her last visit, and the sweet aroma of sap and needles hugged her like an old friend.

"Kate!" From the farthest end of a row of folding tables, a hand shot up in greeting.

She smiled, hurrying toward her friend Harry Marbot, where he sat with three other men playing dominoes. "Are you going to introduce me to your friends?"

Harry pointed to the empty chair next to his. "Sit. Sit."

A quick glance at her watch reminded her that she was due in the laundry room in ten minutes, so she gave him a quick nod. "Just for a bit." She slid onto the metal seat.

With a freckled finger, Harry pointed to each of his companions, calling them by name. "Jess, Jerry, and Tom, this is Kate Matthews."

"It's Kate Sullivan now," she said.

"Oh. Right. You tied the knot a while back." Harry rolled his eyes. "So why are you here? Why aren't you with your new husband?"

"He's working the night shift at the hospital." With a wink, she added, "So where else would I be? I couldn't miss a chance to visit with you."

Harry couldn't have been much over thirty. His eyes were stunningly green, like the color of spring grass. But they were also haunted and wary, as though he'd seen things he'd never be able to forget. Things that lived with him every day. Things that kept him from returning to a world that didn't understand.

A fist squeezed in her stomach, and Kate took a shaking breath.

Stephen hadn't returned to his old world either. Yet there had been no telegram, no missive from the army. Others in their neighborhood had received word of sons and brothers who would never return from the jungles of Vietnam. And some had gotten letters saying only that a loved one was missing in action, which was even worse.

But no news was the worst of all.

Stephen was out there. Somewhere. He'd just never come home. And if he hadn't come home, then maybe he'd ended up in a place just like St. Jude's Mission. So this was where she'd stay. Until she knew he was safe.

Until she finally gave him his ten-year-old Christmas gift.

Maybe she'd never truly understand everything he'd been through, but it didn't change the hole in her heart. Stephen was the only family she had left. She had to find him.

And she prayed it would be by Christmas.

Harry nudged her with his elbow. "Show 'em the picture."

Jerking her bag from the floor, she yanked the image from its spot in an outer pocket, holding it out to each of the men. Foreheads wrinkled and eyes squinted in concentration. But soon the all-too-familiar response began. A slow shake of the head and a gentle frown.

Kate swallowed the lump in her throat and pushed away from the table. "Teresa is expecting me in the laundry room. Those Christmas Eve tablecloths won't iron themselves. But first..." She held up scarves for each of them, and every frown turned to a broad smile, eyes glowing with pleasure.

Such a simple gift. But no man, whether he had a home or not, had ever turned away her yarn and thanks.

Just as Jess took the last scarf, the cafeteria door opened, and another man ambled in. He was older than the domino players by at least a few years, his gray hair trimmed short and covered with a faded gray cap that looked like it belonged on a boy wearing knickers about a hundred years before. Lines framed his face, and stripes of dirt and mud clung to his thin khaki jacket. The blue of his eyes were warm but reserved, and when he caught her gaze, he snatched his hat off his head, twisting it until it had lost all shape.

"Ma'am." His voice was hesitant, and his Adam's apple bobbed in a long pause. "Th...they said I could get a hot meal here."

Oh, Lord. It was the only prayer she could muster when faced with the possibility that Stephen had ended up just like this man. What if he was hungry and dirty and utterly alone in the world? What if he thought he didn't have a home to return to?

Tears pricked at the corners of her eyes, and she tripped over the leg of Harry's chair as she reached a hand out to the newcomer. "Yes. You're a little early for the meal." She paused to inhale the aroma of chicken stew and blueberry cobbler wafting from the kitchen, which was enough to make her own stomach rumble. "But you're just in time for a game." She motioned to the chair she'd just vacated and tried to smile, her lips trembling with the effort. "Please. Take my spot."

The men eyed the new arrival until Jerry stood up. "Davey? Is that you?"

The newcomer nodded quickly. "Jer?"

"Hey!" Jerry's entire face lit up like the Christmas lights that crisscrossed the ceiling. "Davey was my noncommissioned officer in the jungle. I haven't seen you since 1970. Where you been?"

Davey shrugged. "Around."

All the men nodded. That was a sufficient answer to everyone, save Kate. She bit back the myriad questions that battled for release, instead reaching into her bag for another scarf. But the only one left was bright red and still as soft as velvet. The big green bow about its middle had been retied over and over throughout the years, but the ribbon was the same one she'd snuck from her mother's sewing box.

Kate lifted her gaze as Davey slipped into the chair. "I'm afraid I don't have another scarf for you. But I'll get you one. I promise." She looked right into Davey's eyes. "After dinner, if you'll wait, we can see about getting you a different coat."

He looked down at his sleeves as though he'd forgotten he was even wearing a jacket. "Different?"

"Warmer."

Davey's forehead slowly unwrinkled. "All right."

"Good." She reached out to touch his shoulder but stopped before her fingers found purchase. Sometimes men visiting the mission had gone months without physical contact. Sometimes they wanted it that way. "I'll see you at dinner then. Teresa's waiting on me. I better go."

She had already taken three steps when Harry called her back. "Aren't you going to show Davey your picture?"

Her stomach sank. What was the use? No one ever recognized Stephen.

And what if Davey is different?

The voice in the back of her mind refused to be silenced, so she pulled out the photograph, handing it to Davey. "Do you know him?"

His eyebrows pulled together, and his nose wrinkled for several long seconds. When his lids dropped, his eyes kept moving, as if he could see more in the darkness. Finally, his face relaxed into a very slow nod.

Kate's heart stuttered, and her mouth turned into a desert. "You do?"

"I'm pretty sure I shared a fire with him about two weeks ago."

Her legs buckled, and everything went silent except for the roaring of blood rushing to her heart.

Stephen was alive!

And he was in Philadelphia.

Oh, Lord, let me find him. Soon.

KATE SPRAYED STARCH ACROSS A TABLECLOTH before making a second pass with the iron. To her right, Teresa had stopped moving, the clean sheet in her hands only half folded.

"What did Davey say?" Teresa asked. "Does he know where Stephen is?"

Kate shook her head, pressing her lips together. "Not right now. He only saw Stephen that once. Davey said he can't remember where he usually stays. But he promised to tell me as soon as he does."

Teresa's white teeth flashed as she flipped the sheet into submission. "I can't believe he's really here. I mean, that he's in Philadelphia."

"*You* can't?" Kate paused her iron as her heart resumed a thundering pace. "I haven't seen him in ten years, and to know he's so close..." Her throat closed, and she clamped her mouth shut, trying to keep the joy and worry from spilling out.

"Oh, hon." Teresa tossed the linens into a plastic laundry basket and reached out to hug Kate.

While only a few years older than Kate, Teresa reminded Kate of childhood and the warmth of her mother's arms. Kate had lost her mom nearly five years before, but she could still smell the lavender potpourri that had permeated her mom's wardrobe. She could feel the brush of soft fingers at her temples.

And the confusion over her parents' reaction to Stephen's enlistment was as acute as ever.

She couldn't remember her mom without an accompanying knot in her stomach. The feeling took her back to the top of the stairs, peeking through the slats in the railing but covering her ears at her father's every outburst. Raised voices and her mother's pleading.

Kate had been told to go to bed. She wasn't supposed to have heard any of it.

But if she had done what her mom said, she never would have been able to race down the stairs after her father pronounced, "If you're dead-set on joining up,

Stephen, on going against your family's wishes, then don't bother coming back."

She would have missed squeezing Stephen's waist with all the might in her spindly arms and whispering against his soft flannel shirt, "Don't go. Please don't go."

"I have to. But I love you, Katie," he said. As he lifted her chin to look into his face, his gaze had been so blue, so filled with strength and assurance that he was doing the right thing, that she'd almost believed he was. "Always will."

Kate let go of Teresa so fast that it surprised them both, swiping her fingers below her eyes to keep her makeup from smearing.

"Are you going to be okay?" Teresa asked, running a hand through her feathered hair and straightening her sweater.

"As soon as I find him."

Stephen had promised he'd always love her. She could do nothing less for him.

Spreading a red table runner adorned with hand-stitched candles across her ironing board, she set to work before Teresa could drum up any more memories that threatened tears.

"Are we really going to use all of these tablecloths and decorations for the Christmas Eve meal?" Kate asked.

"I'm counting on it." Teresa lifted her basket to her hip. "At least this year."

"What do you mean?"

A frown worked its way across Teresa's lips. "Michael didn't see much use in decking the halls this or any time of the year. He said the men who showed up here weren't interested in anything more than a hot meal, and that was all he was bound to give them."

Kate's blood bubbled, and she slammed the iron on its end with a thump. The mission's former director had lasted just ten months in the role because of that attitude. And if he were still here, she'd give him a piece of her mind.

The men who looked to St. Jude's for help were more than just bellies to be filled. They deserved hope and love. They were someone's family.

"I know." Teresa nodded as though Kate had spoken out loud. "Michael was convinced that our guests end up here because they're lost causes."

"These men are *not* lost causes!" The words exploded from Kate. She clapped her hands over her mouth and glanced over her shoulder to see if her outburst had attracted the attention of the kitchen helpers, who were busy setting up to serve the evening meal, their trays and tins clanking in the next room.

"Well, you don't have to tell me that. I'm not the one who named this place."

St. Jude. The patron saint of lost causes.

Well, no one was going to convince her that helping the wounded souls returning from the rage of war was a lost cause.

Stephen was not a lost cause.

"At least it seems like the new mission director doesn't feel that way," Teresa said. "He's already got his fingerprints all over the way things are running, even though he doesn't start for more than a week."

"What do you mean?"

Eyebrows raised Teresa asked, "Didn't you hear?" She shifted her laundry basket to the other hip with a sigh. "He set a curfew for all the female volunteers. They have to be in by twilight, and they can't go out on mission work at night without at least one male companion. The board of directors liked the new rule so much they implemented it starting today."

Kate shook her head, picking up the steaming iron and taking a thoughtful pass over years of wrinkles. "Who is this guy?"

"Apparently he's former military and has a stack of rules taller than your boots. They've been calling him Gunny."

Kate's brown boots reached nearly to her knees, and she glared at them as though it might make the new director easier to work with.

There were never enough men volunteering at the mission, so the women—in twos and threes—visited small communities below the railroad tracks and near the bridge, taking food and blankets to the people who refused to set foot inside.

And if Stephen was among those not able to find refuge from the snow and bitter winds?

The new director could ruin everything.

IT SEEMED THAT EVERY VOLUNTEER AND MISSION regular pitched in over the next week to turn the cafeteria and common areas into a winter wonderland. While real snow piled up outside the main entrance, paper snowflakes made by local schoolchildren were hung inside from the ceiling. Garland outlined the door frames and red and green table runners had been placed on the dozen folding tables that lined the dining room.

But as Kate tacked an evergreen wreath above the food line two days before Christmas, she felt anything but festive. Her husband was on duty at the hospital every night that week, leaving Kate to focus on the other man in her life. The one she couldn't find.

God, where is he? Her prayers often ran in that vein, but the answer remained elusive. There had been no sign of Stephen, and Davey hadn't returned after his first night.

Kate sighed and rubbed her hands on her blue jeans as she climbed down off the ladder. Maybe it had all been wishful thinking that this year might be different. That this Christmas she would finally be able to give Stephen his scarf.

The ladder wobbled as she reached the middle rung, but a hand on her back caught her before she could stumble. "Whoa, there, Kate."

She smiled over her shoulder, meeting the gaze of the mission's janitor, Melvin Cutter. "Thank you, Mel."

He nodded, shaggy brown hair bouncing, as he helped her down the last couple steps. "That's a tricky step, that one is." As soon as her feet were on the ground, he whisked the ladder away, clearing the path for the men who were already beginning to line up for a feast.

Just as Kate turned toward the kitchen, Melvin called out, "Oh, there was someone looking for you earlier."

"Who?" She spun, forcing down the bubble of hope that insisted on filling her chest and making her breaths come in strange gasps. It could just as easily have been Teresa as someone who recognized her brother.

Melvin scratched his cheek, his fingers rasping against his graying beard. "Don't know that I know his name. He was here last week. Said he met you, but he didn't have one of your scarves. He sure did have a nice coat, though."

The bubble swelled. She'd gotten Davey one of the donated coats last week. Was he finally back? "Was he wearing a gray hat?"

"Yep. He sure was."

She ran for the door, her bell-bottoms swishing as she moved.

"Kate!" Teresa called. "Where are you going? The meal is about to start. We have to serve."

Kate stopped and flicked a glance over her shoulder at her friend. Teresa was right. Her gaze traveled back toward the low hum of male voices waiting for their meal. But if Davey was looking for her, he might have some news.

"I'll be right there," Kate said, holding up a finger.

"What are you doing?" Teresa clapped her hands to her hips, her forehead wrinkling. "The new director is supposed to stop by tonight. We can't start dinner late."

"But Davey..."

"Will still be here after supper is served."

Kate's resolve turned to pudding, and she finally nodded. "All right." She trailed after Teresa, tucking all of her red hair into a hairnet and donning a white apron over her paisley top.

Manning the vat of green beans, Kate doled out a spoonful to each man who passed through the line. She tried to give them a genuine smile too, but her mind kept wandering to the face she hoped to see.

When she scooped out the last of her beans, Kate closed her eyes and shook her head. She'd missed Davey. He hadn't stayed for the meal. He hadn't stayed to tell her his news.

If he'd found her brother, would she ever know?

Tears suddenly gushed to the forefront, and as she carried her empty pan to the kitchen, she didn't look at Teresa or any of the other volunteers. She threw the dish into the sink with a clatter of metal against metal, ripped off her apron and hairnet, and ran for the front door.

The cold stole her breath and gave her life at the same time. She sank onto a bus bench at the corner and lifted her face to the inky sky, where only the tiniest sliver of moon fought its way through the heavy, snow-carrying clouds.

Davey and most likely Stephen would be subject to the elements yet again. They'd spend Christmas Eve with only coats and newspaper to protect them from the snow. Only if they were lucky would they have some kind of roof over their heads.

She'd missed her chance to find them, and the new director hadn't even bothered to show up.

Cupping her hands and blowing into them, she doubled over against the frigid cold, which felt like it was poking slow, painful holes through her. She'd left her coat inside, and now she had just a taste of what these men faced every minute of every freezing night. Men who had spent so many Christmases in a bloody jungle had returned to a country that didn't understand them. So many had chosen addiction and a cheap high, but some were just lost, not sure where home could be found.

"I wanted this Christmas to be special," she whispered, "but I can't do it. I can't find him in time. Maybe this is a lost cause. Forgive me." For missing so many wounded souls. For waiting until her father was gone to begin looking.

For waiting too long.

KATE TRIED TO JOIN IN WITH THE CAROL SINGING the next night, but her voice cracked and her lungs were dry. She had no spirit to give to the holiday, no joy to share with her friends. Turning from the ruddy, smiling faces of the hundred men who would wake up on Christmas morning warm and safe, she focused on the notes on the sheet music in front of her, letting her fingers dance across the keys, finding the familiar melodies of their own accord.

"Angels we have heard on high, sweetly singing o'er the plains." Deep voices, some so far off key they couldn't find the right notes with a map, mingled with the sopranos lilting from the kitchen. The tinkling of silverware being washed added a percussion section, and Kate managed a smile at Harry, his grin broader than the rest.

As she finished the song, Harry pointed toward the back of the room, and her gaze followed his direction until it landed on a familiar face.

Shoving her chair away from the upright piano that had been tuned up just for this occasion, she waved at her singers. "A short break for the accompanist, if you don't mind."

The resounding groans didn't even slow her down as she wove a path toward the man standing by the door, his gray hat wrung into near oblivion, his eyes trained on a spot between his boots.

"Davey. I'm so happy to see you." She reached for his arm, but again stopped before actually making contact. "Merry Christmas Eve."

He nodded, never quite bringing his gaze beyond her knees. "Mer—Merry Christmas to you too."

"I'm sorry I missed you last night." She had to take an exaggerated breath to keep her words from flowing out heedlessly. "Melvin said you were looking for me?"

Another nod. Another long silence while her heart pounded like it would beat right out of her chest.

"Have you seen my brother?"

"Yes. He was under the train tracks. The new ones. 'Bout a mile from here."

"Tha—" Her voice failed, and her only recourse was to swing her arms around his shoulders and hug him with everything she was worth. Every muscle in his body tensed up, his arms freezing between them, but she didn't care. She just squeezed him tighter. "Thank you. Thank you."

As quickly as she'd pulled him into her embrace she let him go, and he swayed on his feet as though they were cemented to the floor. She spun to announce that the music for the evening was over, but Harry, with a decidedly "Chopsticks" style, had already picked up where she left off. She went to find her coat. Oh, and she'd need a blanket and a coat for Stephen.

And his Christmas scarf.

With every thought she fluttered back and forth, her hands wringing and breaths coming in swift gasps.

"You . . . you're not going to look for him tonight, are you, ma'am?"

She skidded to a halt at Davey's hand on her arm, the first time he'd voluntarily touched her. His gaze was wary but steady, concerned.

Patting his fingers, she said, "This could be my last chance. I can't miss it."

"N...not alone."

Her stomach flopped. The new director's rules. She'd have to find a male and a female volunteer to go with her. But there were none to spare. Everyone had a job to do—especially on Christmas Eve. Already cooks were in the kitchen preparing the biggest feast of the year. They anticipated more than twice the usual guests for the turkey dinner. There would be no one willing to just pick up and leave.

But she didn't have a choice.

"If I have to."

As Kate yanked her coat from the hook in the kitchen, Teresa looked up from where she was covering a giant turkey with aluminum foil so that it would be ready to pop in one of the four ovens first thing in the morning. "Where you going?"

"To find my brother."

Teresa's features twisted with confusion. "Tonight? But it's freezing, and it's Christmas Eve."

"Exactly."

"You can't just go. The new director is expected back tonight, and you know about his rules."

Kate fought the ache in her stomach. If she was caught out after curfew, she could be dismissed as a volunteer at St. Jude's. But if she stayed, then she would prove that her search for Stephen—and her love for him—was halfhearted at best.

And that was unacceptable.

Cinching the belt of her coat around her middle, she gave her friend a curt nod. "If he finds out, then so be it. My brother is out there, and I'm not coming back without him."

She stopped just long enough to pick up a blanket and swing her bag of scarves over her shoulder before running through the foyer and slamming into the front door. It gave way, and she stepped onto the sidewalk.

Davey stood directly in her path, his eyes shining and clear and meeting hers confidently. "I could show you the way, if you like."

Her cheeks stung from the cold and the force of her smile. "I'd like that very much." Reaching into her bag, she produced a handsome blue scarf that matched his eyes. "But first, you should put this on."

He wrapped it into place under his chin, repaying her with his smile, toothy and crooked. He turned and hurried down the street, Kate scurrying to match his longer strides.

"We're going to find him, aren't we?" Kate asked breathlessly.

Davey nodded, leading the way through winding blocks, each progressively deteriorated. Lost loved ones and labor strikes had left the big buildings in South Philly wretched guardians of a people longing to prosper. If not for the snow-covered stoops and the occasional string of multicolored lights in a first-floor window, Kate wouldn't have guessed it was Christmas Eve.

After half an hour of walking, Davey said, "Just there."

Under the completed section of railroad tracks, a fire in a barrel lit up a small community of cardboard boxes, and Kate's feet stilled. "Oh, Lord," she whispered, her prayer the only two words she could muster.

Two men stood by the fire, rubbing their hands over the flames. One called out, "Who's there?"

"It's me, Davey. You seen Buddy? He was here this morning."

"He took off."

Kate had never heard such painful words. Not even when her father had dismissed Stephen for deciding that he couldn't remain a pacifist while his friends lost their lives.

Davey's touch was tentative as he set his fingers on her shoulder. "You know where he went?"

"The mission. Said he hoped they'd still have a hot meal."

"St. Ju...ude's?" Her voice tripped on the word as her knees began to buckle.

"Yep."

Davey scooped an arm around her back, and they ran at full speed back the way they'd come. When they turned the corner to the entrance, Kate nearly barreled into Teresa, who was pacing in front of the doors.

"He's here." Teresa's features were drawn tight.

"I know." Kate had to pause to catch another breath. "Stephen is here."

"No. Not Stephen. Gunny. The new director. The gunny sergeant." Teresa put her hands on Kate's shoulders, but Kate just stepped to the side.

"Did you hear what I said? My brother is in there." She nearly danced through the doors, Davey right on her heels, through the foyer and into the dining room, where the singing was only just winding down in favor of pumpkin and apple pie.

"There!" Davey pointed to a tall man with shaggy red hair and a mug in his big hands, and nervous butterflies filled her stomach. Ten years was too long but not long enough to prepare her for this moment.

"Stephen?" she called. Then again, louder. "Stephen!"

Every head turned in her direction, including the redhead, his expression as confused as every other in the room. Below his unkempt whiskers, an unfamiliar frown tugged at his mouth.

She stumbled back, dropping her bag and bumping into Davey as her eyes began to burn. The red hair and freckles were familiar, but this man—Buddy—was not her brother.

"Katie?"

Her entire world tilted on its axis. She couldn't see who had called her name, but she knew that voice. And that only one man had ever called her Katie.

With careful steps she turned to look behind her at the man who must have followed her into the cafeteria. He was tall—well over six feet—and broad, his shoulders stretching the seams of his navy-blue button-up. His shock of red hair was conservatively cut, revealing ears that stuck out just a little bit. But it was his eyes that she knew, that she'd seen in the mirror every day of her life.

She let out a soft cry and ran to him, throwing her arms around his middle as she'd done as a twelve-year-old, holding him just as fiercely.

After a long pause, his arms snaked around her shoulders and his chin rested on top of her head. "Katie, what are you doing here?"

"I've been looking for you." Oh, how she'd waited to say those words, but once they were out, they were utterly insufficient. "I had to find you. I was worried."

"About me?" His words rumbled beneath her ear.

"Of course."

Suddenly the weight of a hundred curious pairs of eyes was too much.

Teresa stepped to Kate's side. "Maybe you'd like to use the director's office for this reunion?"

"Director?"

Stephen nodded in silence, his gaze eating her up, sweeping her from head to toe and back again. Picking up her bag, she followed his urgent steps through the foyer and into the administrative office. Boxes of unpacked pictures and awards sat on the desk and in nearly every chair, so he simply leaned against the metal desk, crossing his arms over his chest.

"What are you doing here? How did you...?" He wore his confusion across every crevice of his face, and she pressed her hands to her mouth to keep too many unidentifiable emotions from erupting.

Through her fingers, she whispered, "I thought you might come here. If you needed help."

His eyes narrowed. "You thought I was homeless." It wasn't really a question, but she nodded anyway. "You thought I'd been broken by the war."

"I didn't know. I just knew you didn't come home. The war's been over for years, and I waited and waited, but you didn't find me."

He shook his head slowly. "I didn't think I had a home to come back to. I didn't think you wanted me to—"

"But I did! I've been looking for you for years. But you stopped answering my letters."

His chin jerked back and forth. "No. You stopped answering mine."

She dug into her bag and produced his picture. "This is the last letter I got from you."

"I wrote you every week that first tour. Katie, I didn't want to leave you or Mom, but Dad made it clear—"

"Dad."

The word came out on a sigh, and Stephen's eyes lit in understanding. Their father, who had espoused peace at any cost, had sabotaged them and their letters. He'd kept brother and sister apart for ten years, but he wouldn't claim another day.

"I'm so sorry," she said.

"I'm so proud of you."

"Of me?"

A grin split his features. "I saw your wedding announcement. In fact..." He dug into one of the nearby boxes and pulled out a wooden frame. Holding it out, he showed off the newspaper clipping from three months before.

"You framed it?"

"It's the most recent picture of you I have." He set the picture on his desk. "So you're a nurse, and you married a doctor."

"Yes. And you? Are you married?"

"Almost. The date is set for this spring."

She'd missed so much of his life, and she wanted to ask him every question racing through her mind. But first she had a present for him.

From the bottom of her bag, she produced the ribbon-tied scarf. "I've been saving this for you."

He released the bow, letting the rich yarn spill across his hands. "How long have you been carrying this?"

"Since you left in 1966."

He laughed, wrapping the scarf around his neck. "And it's still in style. But I don't have anything for you."

"You. You have you. And that's all I ever wanted."

His smile made her heart hurt in an entirely new way because the greatest gift this Christmas was the return of a brother lost.

"All I really wanted was you," she said, then flashed an impish grin at her big brother. "And a piece of pumpkin pie."

A BRACELET FOR
CHRISTMAS

Jacqueline Wheelock

Near the Mississippi Gulf Coast, November 29, 1957

Maureen Wheeler bounced along Highway 63 next to her grandfather in his faded 1946 International Harvester pickup, wondering how much longer it would be before one of the coiled seat springs broke through and bit into her backside. Seeking a safer position, she scooted toward the passenger's window and peered out at the clouds piling in from the west. Cold clouds, Grandma used to call them—that November expanse of billowing gray that promised no rain, only biting temperatures heralding the death of autumn.

Pawpaw Wheeler's arms tensed toward the steering wheel as he frantically pumped the brakes. "Doll Baby, best you quit that daydreamin' now and hold on."

Doll Baby. Ordinarily Maureen cringed at the embarrassing little-girl endearment, but recognizing her grandfather's focused calm as a sign of danger, she braced herself against the dashboard and prepared to join the parents she'd never known in the sweet by-and-by. One eye open and the other squeezed shut in prayer, Maureen gasped an instant before Pawpaw, his brakes screeching desperately, jerked into the oncoming traffic lane to keep from hitting a stalled pulpwood truck.

"Ha! That was a close one, wudn't it, Doll Baby?" asked Pawpaw, clearing the hazardous truck and repositioning himself into the right lane.

Maureen whooshed out a breath of relief. More and more she understood why her eighteen-year-old sister, Elaine, no longer rode with Pawpaw. But Maureen reckoned it was worth the risk one more time.

At nine years old, she still bubbled with anticipation of the game her grandfather played with her this time of year—pretending he'd forgotten what she wanted for her birthday, taking her into town and casually letting her make a wish, then "surprising" her with it for Christmas.

This year, though, Pawpaw had made it clear that the bracelet Maureen couldn't stop jabbering about was more than his salary at the paper mill could support. But like the storms off the gulf that relentlessly carved trenches into the sandpit behind her house, Maureen had a way of wearing down Pawpaw's resolve until she got what she wanted. And she wanted that bracelet more than anything she'd ever wanted in her life.

"Pawpaw?"

"Yeah?"

Maureen paused to study the shivering hood of the old aqua colored truck, the white lie embedded in her latest scheme leaving a scorched imprint on her conscience like an overheated smoothing iron.

"Pawpaw, did I forget to mention that bracelet my friend at school told me about?"

Though pestering her grandfather came as naturally as the dimples in her cheeks when she smiled, never before had Maureen taken to outright lying to him—like she'd been doing lately. Like she was doing right now.

But what else could a girl do? She had to own that fairy-tale bracelet.

"Pawpaw?"

"No, Doll Baby, you didn't forget. Matter of fact, I reckon by now you up to tellin' me about it a dozen times or more."

That many? Maureen pinched her lips into a pout and began a silent prayer for help. And forgiveness.

Now I lay me down to—

Nope, wrong prayer.

Almighty and sovereign Father—

Uh-uh, too much like the preacher's mile-long prayers that coaxed her eyelids toward sleep each Sunday.

All right, Lord. I give. I'm go'n just be plain with You. I'm askin' You to forgive me for halfway fibbing to Pawpaw about my new friend 'til I can at least see this bracelet she been talkin' about.

Guilt clawing at her worse than the aging seat springs, Maureen slunk even closer toward the window and stared at the interminable pines zipping by in the opposite direction. She tugged at one of her five braids and sighed. How could she have guessed—just two measly months ago—that the cherub-faced girl she'd met in the grocery store would turn out to be such a word artist? Why, Ellen Longstreet describing something was like someone taking a tiny brush and swirling the shape and color across your brain. From a slice of lemon meringue pie to a golden Christmas bracelet with red and green rhinestones, Ellen could make a thing so real you'd do almost anything to see it.

Trouble was, Ellen and Maureen didn't attend the same school, as Maureen had led her grandfather to believe. Nor was Maureen likely ever to be accepted as Ellen's best friend. Because Ellen Longstreet was a white girl.

And Maureen was black.

Crossing the river into the coastal town of Moss Point, Maureen watched as the sun broke through the cold clouds, cutting a swath of light across Pawpaw's face. Once again, Pawpaw had skipped his much-needed shave. And now here they were rattling along Main Street with her grandfather looking like an underfed porcupine.

Remembering one of Little Orphan Annie's favorite phrases, she ducked her head and stifled a snicker. *Gee whiskers.*

"What you gigglin' about over there?"

"Nothin'. Except your whiskers showin'."

Pawpaw rubbed his fingertips along his chin, twinkles of mischief dancing inside brown eyes flecked with cloudiness.

"For true? I thought sure last night's shave would do the trick."

"Now, Pawpaw, you know you didn't shave last ni—"

A monster billboard—towering above chubby plastic Santas clinging to light poles and multicolored tinsel dripping from storefronts—arrested Maureen in midthought. She tugged her jacket lapels to her throat as a chill blew hard on her spirits. Never had she seen a polio sign that large. Amidst the glow of the holidays, the pretty little girl with the strapped leg and stilted crutches seemed out of place.

"Wonder why they want to put up that poor little girl in the middle of Christmas?"

Pawpaw rubbed his whiskers again, his weathered face turned serious. "Don't know, Doll Baby. Maybe the town leaders want to remind us not to forget that for every pound of good in this world, there's always at least an ounce o' bad. And too many times, I'm sorry to say, the good ends up on the high side of the scales. But what you got to remember is God works in mysterious ways—"

Maureen's eyes rolled toward the sagging ceiling. *Uh-oh, he fixin' to go to preachin' again.*

"—His wonders to perform."

Oh brother. What in the world did wonders have to do with the little crippled girl on the billboard? What "wonders" could ever come of something like that? Maureen parted her lips to question Pawpaw's own mysterious ways, then promptly felt her mouth forming a perfect O.

Lips quivering with a knowing smile, Pawpaw jerked his relic to a shuddering stop at the curb in front of the jewelry store. The store that held the bracelet that had fastened itself around every one of Maureen's dreams for the last two weeks.

Joy to the world.

She didn't know yet whether Pawpaw meant to buy the bracelet. But allowing her to see it was a step in the right direction. Wild driver though he was, Needham Wheeler was the sweetest pawpaw in Mississippi.

CURTAINED WITHIN A STAND OF PINES DUBBED Ellen's and her secret island, Maureen's heart exulted in the thought of Ellen's face when she saw the bracelet.

She still couldn't believe Pawpaw paid ten dollars for it. Ten dollars! When the ring he'd bought her last year from the five-and-dime had cost a measly fifty-nine cents.

Maureen smiled. She liked the word *measly*. She used it a lot lately because it so ably fit Elaine's new boyfriend and his refusal the other day to offer her a bite of his Baby Ruth.

Minutes ago, she'd wolfed down the ham-seasoned white lima beans and corn bread her sister had prepared without a single taste bud participating. Pretending to choke on the last giant bean, she'd excused herself to the backyard, snatched her celebratory items from underneath the house, and lit out toward the sandpit. Now, drawing her fisted hand from the pocket of her dress, she slowly extended her fingers and gazed with hopeless admiration at the glittering bracelet in her palm.

"*Bee-yoo-tee-full.*"

And wouldn't Ellen be thrilled for her? She hoped so.

Maureen bit into her favorite candy bar and tried to calm herself. She and Ellen had known each other less than two months—ever since the day they'd reached for the one remaining Baby Ruth on a grocery-store shelf at the same time.

"Sorry," they'd said with one voice. "You can have it. No, you take it," they'd both insisted, before releasing a string of snickers.

Leapin' lizards! Could a match have been more perfect? They both had deep dimples. They both were nine. They both liked the funny papers— Little Orphan Annie, to be sure. And they both lived in the same rural settlement twelve miles inland. Perfect. Except Ellen was white and Maureen was black. And although they lived less than a mile apart, one might as well have lived on Mars and the other in China.

But Maureen had quickly found a way around that, suggesting the cover of a circle of pines in the center of the deserted sandpit separating their communities. Each Tuesday since, they'd met here.

Thoughts nose-diving toward the ugly, frightening things she'd recently heard on the radio, Maureen pondered that elusive "color line" Elaine so often spoke of. Elaine was becoming increasingly angry with the way of things, but Pawpaw's mantra remained unaltered: *God works in mysterious ways.*

Maureen had no idea what the color line looked like. But she sure did wonder—even going so far one day as to ask Ellen.

"How you manage to get across that color line without somebody catching you?"

Ellen giggled. "There is no color line, silly. Only in people's hearts. Besides, I can go where I please as long as Daddy doesn't find out."

But Maureen knew better. There had to be a line somewhere. Her sister was a lot of things—bossy being at the top of the list. But she read a lot and she was very smart. And if she said there was a line, there was a line.

Maureen slid the bracelet back into the pocket of her flannel jumper and scanned the island one last time. Her slightly battered tea set, complete with floral croker-sack napkins, was laid out as precisely as the ones she'd seen in magazines. Twinkies and red Kool-Aid had been siphoned from Elaine's kitchen, while the beloved majorette baton Pawpaw had found in a flea market leaned against a pine, itching to be twirled. And then, for the special treat before the unveiling of the bracelet, three Baby Ruths lay atop a syrup can.

Finally seating herself on a stump and primping her hands across her lap, Maureen waited for the code ritual she and Ellen had meticulously formed. Soon, the familiar question from her best friend filled the circle.

"Prettiest li'l girl in the *county-o-o-o-o*?"

"'Cause her pawpaw told her *s-o-o-o*." With gusto, Maureen answered the ditty she'd taught Ellen. "Who goes there in the dead of night?"

"Why, one of the dimpled dancers," retorted Ellen. "And may I ask who goes in there, in the life of day?"

"Why, the only *other* dimpled dancer in the world. Welcome to my party!"

Squealing, Maureen and Ellen locked arms and skipped around the island, moving from clumsy cha-cha steps to the newfangled steps Ellen had garnered from American Bandstand and, finally, to plain old cartwheels.

Ellen, her honey-colored bangs plastered to her forehead, sank into the sand. "I don't feel so good."

Maureen scrambled toward her, nearly tripping on Ellen's sash. "What's the matter? You hungry?" What had Maureen been thinking? Where had her hostessing plan gone? "I bet you about to starve. I'll pour you some red Kool-Aid. That'll get some blood back into your face. Then I've got something—"

But as soon as the liquid touched Ellen's insides, it made its way back up and onto the sand.

"G...got to go."

"But you can't. Not yet. Not until—"

"My legs, they feel funny. I...I want my mama."

Never having seen her own mother, Maureen didn't know how that felt. But one thing was for sure: her lovely bracelet would have to wait.

"I'm goin' with you."

"No, no. You'd better not. My daddy, he might not like it. Might get us both into lots of trouble."

Following Ellen as far as she dared, Maureen looked on helplessly as the winter sun dipped behind the tangle of oaks and myrtles and saw palmetto, while her friend dragged up the north embankment toward the white settlement. What had Pawpaw said? *God works in mysterious ways, His wonders to perform.*

Furiously, she shook her braids. "Uh-uh. God can't be in this."

She'd waited days to show Ellen the bracelet, only to watch her clutch her stomach and sink to the island's floor before Maureen could even begin her party. Unaware of the tears making paths down her chapped cheeks, she smoothed the pocket that held the bracelet.

No. There was nothing wonderful about this. Nothing at all.

"How many times do I have to tell you not to throw that dishwater so close to the steps, Reen?"

Uh-oh. Another of Elaine's sour moods. *Probably got somethin' to do with that stingy boyfriend of hers.* Or could it be that somebody else had gotten hurt crossing that color line? Maureen hung the dripping granite pan on the nail next to the door and placed her hands on what she hoped would one day become a waistline like her older sister's.

"Well then, how come it's all right for you to do it?"

Elaine whirled around from the pan of partly peeled Irish potatoes, her nostrils flaring like a Sunday-go-to-meeting fan—a sign that Maureen was about to best her. Again.

"Why, Maureen Wheeler, I never—"

"*O-o-oh*, yes you did too. I saw you do it more than once, when you was tired and the ground was real dry and you thought nobody was lookin'."

Elaine's shoulders sagged in defeat, her thick, shiny eyebrows drawing inward. Maureen's sister was pretty, even when she was out of sorts.

No wonder that boy stole a kiss.

Elaine's sigh turned into a loving smile. "All right, li'l sister." She wiped her hands on a dishrag and folded Maureen in a hug. "Forgive me for being grumpy. It's just that I heard something today that has me worried about you and all the rest of the children in the settlement."

An unnamed fear feathered Maureen's spine. "Is it about that color line?"

"Not this time. Come on, let's sit down for a minute. Do you know what polio is?"

"'Course I do. Don't everybody?"

"Point taken. It's just that, through the mercy of God, no one in our community has had it before. Till now."

Maureen's stomach cut a flip. She'd not seen Ellen since the day of her friend's strange attack of weakness. And Maureen had been hard pressed to fend off the unfamiliar ailment of worry.

Could Ellen be that sick? *Or maybe she's guessing I got the bracelet 'fore she did and she's mad about it.*

An answer came flying through her lips before she could stop it. "Naw. Ellen ain't like that."

"What?"

"Nothin'. I didn't say nothin'."

"Anyhow, about the polio. I want you to be real careful. No tellin' who else might have it."

A bad feeling washed over Maureen. "You scarin' me, Lainey. What you mean?"

"Well, it probably has nothing to do with us. It happened in the white folks' settlement. In the Longstreet family, I hear. I think they have a little girl—Allie? Ellie?"

A hot poker tore through Maureen's gut. "Ellen. Her name is Ellen. And you best be gittin' it right, you hear me?" She yanked her faded corduroy jacket from the back of a chair. "'Cause she my best friend, and I'm about to go see her. Now."

She dived toward the old splintery back door, its cross boards forming a Z. But Elaine was too fast for her.

"Oh no, you don't. Didn't you hear what I just said? She's got polio. It's contagious. You could become crippled for life, just like President Roosevelt was. Besides, we don't even know where she lives. And you certainly can't cross the color line, traipsing into a white neighborhood by yourself."

"What is a color line? You never do say."

Elaine rattled on as though Maureen's question was posed by a chipmunk. "Supposing someone sees you over there? What're you go'n say? 'Hey, y'all. I just came to check on my best friend'? That community's not safe for you, Reen. Don'tcha understand?"

"Don't care. She my friend, and I'm goin'."

"You go, and I'll tell Pawpaw."

"You do, and I'll tell Pawpaw you let that measly boy kiss you."

"You wouldn't."

"Will too."

Elaine chewed on her bottom lip and moved away from the door. Once more, Maureen had won over her sister in the game of blink. But this time it didn't feel so satisfying. Deep down she knew how much Elaine loved her, how hard she tried to be her mother.

"Okay," Elaine said. "I'll probably never forgive myself for this. Be careful and run like the dickens if somebody gets mean."

CLUTCHING TO HER CHEST *HOW THE GRINCH STOLE Christmas*, Maureen stomped around the special island that had once been so much fun. Minutes ago, back there in the kitchen, she'd been as tough as Wilma Rudolph. But sneaking into a white neighborhood she'd never even seen before might be scarier than running track. Still, ever since the word *polio* had rolled off Elaine's tongue, Maureen had felt like an army of ants had crawled into her stomach, leaving her with waves of fear and loneliness like she'd never before experienced.

Halting her circuit, she looked down at the shiny new book she'd borrowed from the bookmobile. She was too old for Dr. Seuss, and she knew it. But as soon as she'd stepped inside that magic world on wheels last week and flipped through Dr. Seuss's latest book, she'd been hooked on the pure gumption of that town that saved Christmas.

"Humph. That old polio. A Grinch if I ever saw one."

She thought of Ellen's dimples and unwittingly formed her own. No way was Mr. Polio Grinch going to steal Ellen's Christmas. Not as long as her name was Maureen Diane Wheeler.

THE COASTAL WINDS HAD DIED ALONG WITH the sun. Maureen's hands shook so violently that she thought the rattling of the paper from her Blue Horse notebook would wake up the neighborhood. Still, she'd crafted that first note—in cursive, no less—and deliver it she would. Skulking along the manicured lawns of japonicas, magnolias, and sweet gums, she looked for the infamous color line. How would it look? Would it be at the edge of the neighborhood, or would each family have its own—painted over its door like Passover blood in the story in the Bible? And what colors would they choose? Bright, dark, or in between?

She strained to read her note one last time. Writing that note had been the first time Maureen had wished she'd studied her spelling more.

Dear Dempled Dancer Number 2,

I miss you. I have some wunderful news. A sircus in New Orleens is lookin for two dempled dancers. They don't care whut color they are. But they must have demples in both cheeks. Do you know anybody lik that? (Smile.) If you do plese write back and let me know wen you are ready to praktis. I love you my bestest friend.

> Yurs truly,
> Dempled Dancer Number 1

P.S. This note is really mak believe

Dabbing the note with Blue Waltz perfume, Maureen stuck it between two planks of the porch with the Longstreet mailbox in front and disappeared toward the pit.

Over the next few weeks, she wrote more notes. Sometimes she left one before school. Others she sneaked away at lunchtime, hoping the teacher wouldn't miss her. Still other times she waited until Pawpaw's snoring covered any and all sounds from home to Moss Point and trusted the light of the moon to get her to the sandpit's other side. When it rained, she wrapped her notes in wax paper—notes that ran a spread from Maureen's penciled rendition of Little Orphan Annie to her carefully wrapped package of ten Hershey's Kisses—and put them in the country-style mailbox at the edge of the road.

But not once had her notes been good enough to garner an answer. Not one little peep.

MAUREEN PUSHED HER YELLOW SPELLING BOOK to the edge of the kitchen table and gazed out the window into the steamy air. Almost three weeks had passed since she began her forays into the neighborhood on the other side of the sandpit. The bookmobile had come and gone, forcing her to return *How the Grinch Stole Christmas*. Still she'd received no response.

"I wish we had us a television," Maureen said.

Elaine released a long sigh of disapproval. "Reen, you are one lazy li'l dreamer." Yanking one of Maureen's thick braids, she slid a bowl of dried peas in front of her. "Here. If you won't study your spellin' lesson, maybe I can get you to sort through these peas."

Maureen pulsed with confusion and resentment. She really didn't want to fight with her sister today. "Could you just leave me alone?"

"Aw, c'mon, now, Reen. Pickin' a few rocks out of dried black-eyes can't be that bad."

Maureen jerked her fisted hands toward her midriff, dragging a splinter from the worn table underneath her skin. "Ouch!"

Elaine dropped her dishrag and hurried to where Maureen sat. "Lemme see that. Does it hurt bad, Doll Baby?"

Suddenly Maureen's heart hurt much more than the splinter. It was the "Doll Baby" that did it. While Maureen half-loved, half-hated when Pawpaw—who just wanted her to stay little—used her pet name, when Elaine called her that, her sister became the closest thing to a mother Maureen had ever known. And here she was putting herself in the devil's path every day by not only going into a neighborhood that was as foreign as Chicago, but keeping it from the two people who loved her more than anything. Traitorous tears slid down Maureen's face as she risked a glance at her sister.

"Reen? Why you cryin'?" Suddenly Elaine's eyes narrowed with understanding. "Oh, Reen, no. Please don't tell me you still tryin' to see that li'l girl with the polio." Elaine's face went from pleading to near panic. "Why, yes you are, ain'tcha! I declare you're gonna be in some kind of trouble when Pawpaw finds out. And I *am* go'n tell him this time. I just hope you don't catch polio before you catch the whippin' you deserve."

Maureen bolted upright in her chair and stuck out her chin. "Pawpaw ain't go'n whip me. Pawpaw ain't never whipped us. He done got on to us 'bout some stuff, but we ain't got no whippin' since Granny died, and you know it."

"Girl, haven't you been listening to the radio and all the stuff that's been happening in Little Rock and places all over the south? Folks gettin' dogs sicced on them, clubs laid up side their heads, jail time—all kinds of bad things. Just because they went where they weren't wanted."

Clearly Elaine was trying to scare her socks off. Sinner though she was, if God really did perform wonders as Pawpaw said, Maureen needed one now.

Lord, just because me and Ellen cut a jig once in a while don't mean we don't love You. And we like You too—all the flowers and Christmas decorations and the special island You gave us. So why me and Ellen being double-Grinched like this with polio and Elaine's color line? Color can't be that important to You 'cause the Grinch is one ugly green, and You gave him a new heart. Please help us. Amen.

Maureen opened her eyes to a softened face.

"Oh, come here." Elaine leaned over and kissed her forehead. "It's go'n be okay. Just promise me you won't go back across that sandpit again. Okay?"

Maureen nodded her assent, eight of her fingers crossed behind her back with both thumbs down the middle. But she knew finger-crossing was just a child's game. Plus the Lord was never going to listen to a hopeless, unrepentant liar like she was. So she might as well do what her heart said was right and not even try to pray.

SIX DAYS BEFORE CHRISTMAS, SHE SAW WHAT her heart longed for. There, carefully folded and taped to one of the porch's pillars, was a sliver of white. A fluttering scary wonderful note written in perfect cursive.

> Dear Maureen,
>
> Thank you for the gifts. A certain young lady who goes by "Dimpled Dancer Number Two" might be getting a new leg bracelet for Christmas. Not to worry, though. God bless you.
>
> E. Longstreet

Why did Ellen say not to worry?

Maureen's spirit soared. Then dipped. Then soared again. Suddenly, she knew what she had to do. She would make her last five offerings very special. After all, Maureen was the only person who really knew what her friend cherished most. Laughter gurgled like a summertime spring.

"Leapin' lizards!"

The Grinch had lost again.

GLANCING OVER HER SHOULDER, MAUREEN lined up her five most valuable possessions on her fold-away cot and wrapped them in colored scraps left over from the Christmas play. The unopened bag of jacks Elaine had purchased for her birthday. Her precious majorette baton. Her first and only pair of bobby socks. A sketch of the special island.

On Christmas Eve, that most happy day when God was nigh to placing Baby Jesus in the manger, Maureen would give her friend the best she had.

Her beloved Christmas bracelet.

She'd quickly figured out why Ellen had said not to worry. Maureen knew how badly Ellen had wanted the Christmas bracelet. The "leg bracelet"—whatever that was—that Ellen's parents were buying was surely well intentioned, but Maureen knew what Ellen had truly wanted for Christmas, and she prayed a place in her heart was still reserved for the Christmas bracelet.

MAUREEN STOOD AT THE STEPS OF THE Longstreets' porch, fingering the bracelet in her pocket and admiring the multicolored lights of the cedar tree showing through the picture window. Finally, Christmas Eve. The last few days had been long, the sun plodding across the wintry skies as though it pulled a load of lead. She'd prayed fervently for a response from Ellen but received nothing. What was she doing wrong? Didn't Ellen like even one of the gifts she'd left?

The idea of knocking on Ellen's door crashed upon her like a Sputnik gone wild. Why hadn't she thought of this before? Emboldened by the thank-you note she'd received, Maureen pulled back the Longstreets' screen door and rapped on the bare wood. After only a few seconds, a woman opened the door.

"Good evening. Maureen, is it?"

Bowled over by how much Ellen's mother looked like her, Maureen stepped back and gazed at the woman's pretty smile. It occurred to her that the sashes had probably come loose from her dress. And her hair. She'd not even waited until Elaine could comb and replait it. Never interested in her appearance before, she suddenly felt poorly dressed.

Recalling the manners Elaine had hammered into her, she mustered up a voice.

"Y...yessum. I...I g...got somethin' for Ellen. C...can I see her?"

The smile of seconds ago faded into a flat line. "I'm sorry, but no."

"But I have to—I mean—I have to save Ellen's Christmas. And I got just the thing. I know I do."

"Now, listen here—" The woman shifted her slim figure toward the door frame.

Behind her, leaning in the corner of the small hardwood entryway, was a brace. Not the dainty leg bracelet

Maureen had imagined but a hard, ugly contraption like the pretty girl on the billboard wore.

A plea slipped past her trembling lips. "Please, ma'am, can—I mean—*may* I see her?"

Mrs. Longstreet hugged herself and looked at the skies. "Now, you just run along home. The weather's turnin' nasty, and I'm sure your mama's wonderin' where you are. Besides, Mr. Longstreet's waitin' for his supper."

Suddenly all the horrible images Elaine had warned her about flooded Maureen's mind. All true, all staring her in the face. Ellen's mother didn't like her just because she was different. Maureen might not have found the color line yet, but in that instant, and for the first time, she felt strangled by an invisible rope choking life and hope from her.

Quietly she placed the bracelet next to the woman's feet, then changed her mind and quickly snatched it up again before fleeing into the darkest Christmas Eve night she had ever known.

SITTING ON THE WINE-COLORED STUDIO COUCH near Pawpaw's decorated holly tree, Maureen stared out over the frozen yard. Though the rare overnight icicles glistened like diamonds against the green of the live oaks, Christmas morning was as bleak as last evening's nightmare.

Elaine bustled into the front room doing her best to spread cheer. "Doll Baby, you ain't go'n believe what Pawpaw done gone and bought for you this time."

Maureen tried to act interested. "What?"

Elaine grinned. "Now, why would I tell something this big to a pipsqueak like you and spoil all the squealin' and jumpin' up and down you go'n do when you see it?"

But though Maureen tried hard, even the new television Pawpaw stood next to did nothing to melt the iceberg covering her heart. The pain of never again playing with Ellen was worse than any toothache she'd ever had. The Grinch had won after all.

Maureen flew to her cot behind the dividing curtain and sank to her knees. *Oh, Lord. Is Ellen even go'n be able to ever dance again? Baby Jesus, I know this Your birthday, but You all grown up now. Can't You please perform one of them wonders Pawpaw always talkin' about? If You would help my friend—even if the color line won't let us play no more—I promise I'll study my spellin'. And I won't sneak Baby Ruths under my bed. And I'll be a neat li'l girl from now own. I'll clean up the kitchen and—*

A soft knock mixed itself with the noise from the television. Pawpaw slung his I-don't-want-to-be-bothered answer toward the door. "Who dat?"

A different kind of drawl from the ones in the black neighborhood seized Maureen's attention.

"Uh, this is John Longstreet. Just wonderin' if I could have a word with ya."

"Well, uh—I'll be right there."

Maureen leaped from her knees and peered from behind the curtain. Elaine shot from the kitchen while Pawpaw jammed gnarled toes into broken-down slippers and shuffled to the door. On the rickety downhill porch boards stood a man holding someone wrapped in a blanket.

"Y'all come on in," Pawpaw said, stepping back to make room.

Ellen called out from the blanket. "Maureen! It's me! I brung you somethin'."

Maureen launched herself out from behind the curtain but stopped short of throwing herself at her friend the way she wanted. They grinned at each other like fools.

"*Brought*, darlin'. The word is *brought*." Maureen recognized Ellen's mother's voice just before she entered the house behind her husband.

Pawpaw waved toward the tiny front room, his high-pitched words sounding watery. "It's pretty nippy out there. Y'all come in and sit down. We was just about to break bread." Pawpaw's cloudy eyes lit up as Mr. Longstreet settled Ellen into a chair. "Would y'all—I mean to say—we don't have a lot, but you welcome to what we have."

"Oh no. We just wanted to deliver something to your—granddaughter. Though I hafta say it smells mighty fine in here." Ellen's father removed his hat and dragged his fingers through hair the same color as Ellen's. "You see, my wife Eliza's a bit worn out from all that's happened these last weeks. She cooked our Christmas dinner last night. We haven't had a chance to warm it up yet, so—"

"John!"

"Well, I only meant—"

Pawpaw laughed out loud. "I know what you meant. You hungry, and I'm sho hopin' y'all stay and eat—that is, if Miz Longstreet don't mind." Pawpaw addressed only Mr. Longstreet, somehow seeming to fear speaking to his wife.

"Please, Mama?" begged Ellen.

Mrs. Longstreet sighed resignedly. "Well, I reckon it'd be all right."

"Lainey, bring in them extry foldin' chairs," said Pawpaw. "And Doll Baby, stop standin' there like you ain't been raised and find your friend some pillows to sit on."

Her *friend*? Maureen felt her eyes stretching to the size of a robin's egg.

Pawpaw winked. "Been knowin' all along. Just waitin' for you to tell your old pawpaw about the latest wonder God's been performing. He do so many, you know, 'til we can't keep up with Him." He pointed toward the table next to the window. "All right, let's pray and eat."

"Wait!" Maureen shouted. "Wait, everybody."

She disappeared behind the curtain and emerged with a gift in her hands. Feeling unusually shy, she studied the mottled flowers of the ancient linoleum.

"I...I got somethin' for Ellen." Voice crackling, Maureen struggled to speak. "Oh, Ellen. I...I miss you real bad. I can't figure out why God ain't go'n ever let us d...dance together again."

Ellen smiled. "What're you talkin' about, Dimpled Dancer? We most certainly will."

"B...but I thought..." Maureen risked a glance at Ellen's mother, who seemed a bit perplexed. "I thought the color line...and, and I saw it last night too. I saw the leg bracelet you wrote about."

Mrs. Longstreet clamped her hand over her mouth, tears springing from her eyes. "You saw that brace? Oh, honey, I'm so sorry. I'd only placed it there to remind myself to return it. The doctor just wanted us to know what it looked like—just in case. Turns out, our Ellen has a mild case and won't be needin' it after all. Why, she's not even infectious anymore."

Maureen squinted. "Infectious? What's that?"

Elaine rushed in with her knowledge. "That just means you could have caught it from Ellen like Ellen caught it from somebody else."

"Which is why you couldn't come in, Maureen," Mrs. Longstreet explained. "We didn't want you to have polio too. And by the way, I'm the one who wrote the note to you."

Dimples flashed all around as Maureen hugged Ellen and placed her gift atop the lap blanket.

Ellen loosed her hand from the folds of the blanket and handed Maureen a tiny package. "I love you, and we shall dance again soon."

Sniffles pierced the silence as the girls unwrapped their gifts.

There, gleaming in the shadows of the tiny room, were identical Christmas bracelets. The girls shrieked and laughed and hugged each other again while their families looked on. God had indeed performed another wonder.

THE FAMILY QUILT

Mona Hodgson

Cripple Creek, Colorado, December 1899

A festive red-and-green plaid ribbon wove through the pine branches that bedecked the parlor mantel. Patsy Michaels tucked herself into the armchair, then lifted the floral teacup from its saucer. In an attempt to relax, she breathed in the sweet aroma of orange and cinnamon.

Teatime at Miss Hattie's Boardinghouse always proved to be pleasurable, but today Patsy felt the mantel clock taunting her as it ticked away precious time. She'd only returned to Cripple Creek two weeks ago, following her father's passing. And she'd brought her mother from Denver to live with them.

According to the hands on the clock, her three children would arrive home from school in less than one hour. Lydia didn't work at the dress shop on Thursdays, so she could help prepare supper while Ruth pulled the clothes from the racks in front of the fireplace and put them away. Joseph could carry in more wood before seeing to his reading assignment. *But,* Patsy reflected regretfully, *I should have cut the vegetables and cooked the stew meat before I left the house.*

Patsy's mother sat on the ornate settee across from her, picking a piece of lint from the skirt of her mourning gown. Mother had been so receptive to Miss Hattie's invitation that Patsy couldn't very well have said no to the teatime diversion.

"I'm happy you were able to come for a visit today, Cora." Miss Hattie's blue-gray eyes shimmered with sincerity as she spoke to Mother. "I am going to like having you so close."

Patsy lowered her cup to the saucer. Perhaps she hadn't made a mistake taking Mother away from the house, friends, and city that had been her home for half of her sixty-two years. If only Christmas was more than two and a half weeks away. She wasn't at all ready to face a holiday, let alone welcome it. Patsy took another faltering breath of orange and cinnamon.

"You were kind to invite us. Thank you." Mother tucked a stray white curl into the low coiffure at the nape of her neck and opened her mouth as if to say more, but pressed her lips together instead.

"You're certainly quiet today, Patsy dear." Hattie smiled. "Harlan might say it was because I'm not letting you get a word in sideways."

Patsy shook her head, giving thought to an answer, when Mother straightened against the back of the settee. "I'm afraid bringing me into the household has caused quite a stir at Patsy's house."

"I've tasted your cooking and seen your stitchery, Cora dear. Having your help around the house is sure to be a boost."

"Not when I can't even muster the energy of a sloth." Mother's flat tone made Patsy's heart ache.

Miss Hattie's eyes brimmed with compassion. "Sorrow sickness."

"*Sorrow sickness*?" Mother echoed Patsy's silent contemplation.

"Yes." Their hostess patted Mother's knee. "But you'll get stronger and the sickness that comes with sorrow will pass."

"Miss Hattie is right, Mother. It is good to have you with us." She couldn't bear the thought of Mother being alone in that house...so far away. Patsy longed to make the adjustment easier on her mother, but how? She couldn't bring Pop back to life, and that's all Mother wanted for Christmas.

The sound of a door opening and closing at the back of the house drew their attention to the parlor door.

"That'll be Harlan back from the parsonage for a visit with Baby Isaac." A sweet pucker bunched Miss Hattie's cheeks. "And a visit with Ida too, of course."

Harlan Sinclair stood in the doorway looking quite stately in a frock coat and vest. A quilt draped his arm, most of it wrapped in a bedsheet. "Music to my ears, the sound of women enjoying one another's company."

"Then you just missed a symphony." Tittering, Miss Hattie set her saucer on the table and fairly floated toward her husband of one year.

He doffed his derby, a smile lifting the corners of his mustache. "Ladies."

Patsy and Mother both returned his greeting.

Miss Hattie stood in front of him. "You brought me a quilt?"

"Yes. From Ida." He gave Hattie a sweet peck on the cheek. "Apparently, Etta Ondersma spoke with you about repairing it?"

Nodding, Miss Hattie pulled the sheet back, revealing a faded Star Block. "Etta left it with your daughter instead of bringing it to me?"

"Ida said that sort of thing is a common occurrence. Apparently, the parsonage serves some ladies as a post office."

"As if that poor girl doesn't have enough to do." Miss Hattie turned to Patsy and her mother. "Etta's grandmother made the Civil War Stars quilt, and she wants to present it to her niece for Christmas."

A thought twirled in Patsy's brain. *A quilt.* What if she and her daughters made one for Mother? A crazy thought, to add yet another task to her already bulging list of them, but she liked the idea of creating a new quilt for Mother's new life.

Patsy drained her teacup. After she and Mother had expressed their thanks and said their good-byes, Patsy followed Mother down the snowy walkway to the blanketed dirt road. The sun was making a rare appearance today, but the air didn't seem to hold its warmth well. Patsy tugged on the sleeves of her woolen mantle while Mother tightened the black scarf at her neck.

Patsy gave Mother's hand a squeeze as they stepped across a muddy wheel track. Several children wandered up the street from the school. But only two of them were hers. Ten-year-old Joseph waved in greeting. Ruth, recently turned fourteen, walked a jagged line behind him, chattering with a girlfriend.

Where was Lydia? Thursday wasn't her usual day to work. But perhaps Vivian, Lydia's employer, had sent a message to Lydia at school. Lydia had said the dress shop was enjoying a brisk business, especially with the Christmas ball fast approaching.

Patsy returned her son's wave and waited for them at the street's edge in front of the house.

Mother gave the children a halfhearted wave. "I'll be inside."

"All right. We'll be in soon."

Joseph reached Patsy first, rosy cheeked, his blond hair askew. Ruth lagged behind, her braid draped over her shoulder.

"Where is Lydia?" As soon as the question gushed out, Patsy chided herself for not greeting them first. "How was school?"

"Fun. Miss Brewster brought a dead frog to school and I got to—"

"Lydia will be along soon." Ruth wasn't a fan of frogs or biology lessons.

Joseph stacked his hands against his chest. "Lydia saw Ar...ch...ie and couldn't take another step."

"Oh?" Patsy directed the question to Ruth.

"We crossed paths with Archie. He was on a package delivery for his father and stopped to greet us."

"Lydia, mostly." Joseph fluttered his eyelashes with the tip of a finger under his chin.

Ruth's gaze narrowed as she fixed it on her brother. "Lydia and Archie were visiting, so we came on home."

"Good." Not good that Lydia was *visiting* with Archie Carlson, because she was needed at home, but good the other two were here. "Joseph, after a bit of refreshment, I need you to bring in more wood for the fire. And, Ruth, the clothes on the rack in the parlor should be dry by now so you can put them away. I didn't hang them outside this morning for fear of another storm." Thankfully, the clouds had cleared.

Joseph glanced from Patsy's leather high-button boots to her black-and-green steamer hat. "Where were you?"

Patsy looked across the street at the gabled yellow boardinghouse. "Gram and I were at Miss Hattie's for tea."

A sigh lifted the loose strands of auburn hair at Ruth's forehead. "Gram probably went right in to rest."

"Yes." Because of sorrow sickness. "You'll find a plate of applesauce cookies on the sideboard. One each, then tend to your tasks before supper."

Joseph climbed the front steps two at a time.

Patsy followed Ruth into the house. Her gait slow, Patsy turned at the parlor and stepped around the clothes rack to add another log to the fire. Her husband, Warren, would be home from the bank after a bit, and liked to sit in the parlor listening to Joseph read.

On Patsy's way past the blue spruce adorned in red ribbon and wooden thread spools, her gaze settled on the carved wooden angel dangling from an eye-level branch. The string had slipped and the poor cherub appeared to be falling headlong toward the earth. Patsy sighed. The suspended ornament captured how she felt: suspended between life and death. Trapped between letting go of her beloved father, trying to cheer Mother, being an attentive wife, raising her children well, and moving on...to celebrate Christmas. If Warren and the children hadn't decorated in her absence, the house would've been as devoid of celebration as her heart felt.

Ten minutes later, the angel back in its rightful place, Patsy stood at the kitchen stove. She'd peeled and cut the carrots and potatoes she'd pulled from the root cellar. Stirring the vegetables into the stew, she tried to slow her thoughts to a simmer. The other two children had been home nearly thirty minutes now. Where was Lydia? This wasn't a good time for Lydia to be distracted. Patsy needed her. Her frustration threatening to boil over, she added salt to the pot.

"Mama?" Lydia was home.

"I'm in the kitchen."

"There you are." Lydia practically skipped into the room. Her daughter's broad smile only added to Patsy's frustration.

She gave the stew a brisk stirring. "Where else would I be this time of day?"

Lydia pulled an apron from the hook and slipped it over her head. At the sink, she primed the pump and washed her hands. "I'm sorry I'm late."

A deep breath seemed to do little to settle the irritation tensing Patsy's shoulders. "You think talking to a boy is more important than helping me."

Lydia's eyes widened. Her smile gone, she pulled six supper plates from the shelf and stacked forks, knives, and spoons. "I didn't mean to upset you."

Thinking she might have to bite her tongue, Patsy slid the pan of biscuits into the oven.

"We saw Archie, and I stopped. I walked with him to deliver a package." Lydia blew out a breath, something she did to quell her own frustration. "We started talking, and time got away from me."

Patsy faced her daughter. "You know," she said, near a whisper, "I have added work on me with Gram here."

"Maybe I shouldn't have stopped to talk to Archie, but he asked to escort me to the Christmas ball. In two weeks and two days."

Patsy's insides clenched. Two weeks? Two years would be too soon. "No."

"It is short notice. Archie apologized for that. Said it took him too long to ask. But it won't be any trouble." Lydia clasped her hands as if to beg.

Patsy busied herself pulling a bread basket from the shelf.

"I'm sure Vivian has a gown I could borrow, so we wouldn't have to think about that."

"I need your help around here. There is no time for balls and all the fuss that accompanies them."

"Why are you punishing me? I took on added work while you were gone. And when you returned with Gram, I moved out of my room and onto the back porch." She rubbed her arms as if to stave off a chill. "And I stumble into Gram's trunk full of old clothes every night trying to get to my bed."

Footsteps pulled Patsy's gaze to the doorway where Mother stood, her face slack.

"Gram!" Pale, Lydia took slow steps toward her grandmother.

"I came in to help." Mother pulled the stack of plates from the countertop.

"I was upset. I didn't mean—"

"The truth is the truth, dear." Mother ambled to the door carrying her burden.

"I'm sorry." Tear pooled Lydia's eyes.

It seemed that was all anyone in the family could say the past several months.

Lord God, please help us.

THE KITCHEN CLEAR OF THE SUPPER DISHES, Patsy sat in the wingback sorting through her sewing basket. It felt good to have a sewing project at hand, even if the timing was crowded. Uncharacteristically silent, the family had made short work of the evening meal. The only two members who seemed to have anything to say were Warren and Joseph, whom she'd silenced when father and son arrived at the topic of the teacher and her frog. Now, Patsy and Warren sat in the parlor in front of a crackling fire, her with the sewing basket and him reading *The Cripple Creek Crusher.*

"Patsy?"

She lifted her gaze to the armed chair across from her. Warren lowered the newspaper to his lap.

"I wish you had talked to me about the Christmas ball before telling Lydia she couldn't go."

"She went to you with complaints about my decision?"

"I went to her. I don't think she said five words at supper, and if her chin had been any lower, it would have taken up table space." Warren brushed his fingers through the silver-tinged hair at his temple. "The three weeks you were gone, Lydia saw to everything here. Cooked and cleaned, looked after Joseph. She deserves an opportunity to socialize a bit."

Patsy couldn't argue with that. She'd been proud of the way Lydia had stepped up to manage the household in her absence.

"Archie Carlson is a good boy, Patsy. A fine young man, I daresay."

She studied a strip of bric-a-brac in the basket. "It's not Archie."

"Then why were you so quick to say she couldn't go? It's just a dance."

Patsy raised an eyebrow and cleared her throat.

"Oh!" A sudden blush colored Warren's face and neck. "Our first kiss happened when I took you home from a Christmas ball." He brushed a finger against his lips. "A delicious kiss, at that."

Patsy swatted at him, fighting a smile. "Lydia is not ready."

Warren's blue eyes narrowed. "Or you're not ready for her to be ready?"

"I saw the spark in her eyes when she spoke of him and his invitation."

"She cares for him, so you said no?"

Put that way, her decision sounded rather impetuous. And selfish.

"Think more about letting her go, will you?"

"I will. While I also think about"—she lowered her voice to a whisper—"how to make life a bit more merry for Mother."

"Your mother will be all right, and you will be too."

"Even if Archie wins Lydia's heart?"

"Yes." His crooked smile sent shivers down her spine despite the warmth from the fireplace.

Patsy closed the flap on her sewing basket. No more time for such contemplations. She and the girls had a quilt to make. And the one good thing that came out of her sour encounter with Lydia and Mother was that Patsy knew exactly what would make the quilt extra special.

A newly found purpose powered her steps past the dining room and through the kitchen toward Lydia's cramped bedchamber on the back porch.

HUDDLED AROUND MOTHER'S OPEN TRUNK IN the glow of lantern light, Patsy and her two daughters pulled out old clothes. "We'll need enough scraps to cover Gram's double bed."

"This is going to be so fun." A smile lit Ruth's eyes, blue like her father's. She pulled a faded blue striped shirt with a high collar from the trunk.

A sweet memory tugged at Patsy. "I patched that shirt for Pop after he caught the sleeve on a fence post nail."

"Gram is going to love her new quilt."

"Or it could be the worst present. What if every time she sees the quilt, it reminds her that Pop is gone?" Lydia's mood hadn't improved any since the conversation about Archie.

Patsy pressed her lips together. Every breath Mother took without Pop beside her reminded her of his absence. But what if Lydia was right? What if a memory quilt was a bad idea, and only made Mother's sorrow sickness worse?

Ruth held the shirt to her nose and breathed in. "Nonsense. Doesn't the Bible say that happy memories are good medicine?"

A giggle bubbled in Patsy's throat. "'A merry heart doeth good like a medicine.'"

Ruth folded Pop's shirt, leaving the patched arm prominent. "Well, we don't have an excess of merry hearts here, so we will have to make do with happy memories."

"I hope you're right." On her knees, Lydia bent over the trunk.

Patsy squirmed on the rag rug beneath her. She should say something more to Lydia about the

Christmas ball, but she couldn't think about that right now. "We need to decide on a pattern."

Lydia pulled Pop's Union uniform trousers from the trunk. "What about a Nine Patch?"

The basic pattern Mother used to teach Patsy to quilt when she was ten. "Perfect."

A smile played on Lydia's face.

Patsy pulled a peach-colored silk damask dress onto her lap and caressed the lace collar. "Gram wore this when your father and I wed."

"See?" Ruth said. "Happy memories!"

Her throat tight with emotions, Patsy nodded and added the dress to the striped shirt and Union trousers.

By Saturday afternoon, all of the squares were cut. Patsy had enlisted Miss Hattie's help in keeping Mother occupied for a couple of hours during the day while she and the girls continued piecing and stitching the blocks. Hattie had summoned a buggy to transport Mother back and forth with her to the Women for the Betterment of Cripple Creek Christmas Luncheon, so that should make detecting Mother's return home effortless. But just in case the slap of hooves on the slushy road wasn't enough, now that two hours had passed, Patsy assigned Joseph to keep watch from the front yard.

Ruth had claimed the rug in front of the sofa and spread her squares and spools of thread around her like chicks encircling a mother hen. Lydia preferred the armed rocker, while Patsy worked at the game table in the corner.

"Gram didn't want to talk about it, but this morning I was finally able to explain my comments from the other day." Lydia looked up from her needlework. "She said she understood."

"She no doubt does. Everything is different for her too."

Lydia's nod bobbed the deep auburn curls dangling at her neck. "And now that we're using the old clothes for her gift and the trunk for storing her surprise, I like having it in my bedchamber."

Patsy couldn't stop the sigh rising out of the second thoughts she'd been having. "I've been thinking. What if Gram is upset because we used the clothes that held so many memories for her? What if the quilt pushes her into a grievous state of nostalgia?"

Lydia added more thread to her needle. "Ruth is right, Mama. The reminder of the good memories is sure to bring Gram joy. I only said those things because I was angry."

"And you're no longer angry with me?"

"I'm still disappointed about not being able to attend the Christmas ball with Archie. But no, I'm not angry with you."

The front door banged open and Joseph skidded to a stop just inside the parlor. "Someone's coming."

Patsy stood. "Who is it?"

"Mrs. Michaels?" The broad smile on Lydia's face confirmed that the voice belonged to Archie Carlson.

"Probably a package delivery. I'll take care of it." Patsy hadn't looked away before seeing Lydia's frown. "We don't have much time left before Gram returns."

"Mrs. Michaels? Lydia? Are you here?"

Patsy closed the parlor door behind her. The young man stood beside the open door. Eighteen now, Archie had done some growing up. His lanky frame had filled out and his shoulders had broadened. "I'm sorry I kept you waiting."

"Good afternoon, Mrs. Michaels. I didn't mean to disturb you."

She gazed at his empty hands. Were they trembling? "There's no package?"

"No, ma'am." He clasped his hands behind his back. "I wondered if I might speak with you."

"Of course." She'd promised Warren she'd think about Archie's invitation and her hasty decision. And now it seemed time had run out.

"Again, my sympathies for your loss, ma'am."

"Thank you."

"This may not be the best time, but…" Archie moistened his lips and squared his shoulders. "Two days ago, I invited Lydia to join me for the Christmas ball. I would come for her in my father's surrey and see her home at a decent hour."

"It's short notice."

"It is. But if it's not too much of an inconvenience, Mrs. Michaels, I hope you'll let her go with me."

Patsy drew in a fortifying breath. "Yes."

"Yes?" Lydia rushed to her side.

Patsy faced her daughter. "Yes, you may attend the ball with Archie as your escort." She shifted her attention to Archie. "You are to have her home no later than ten o'clock."

"Yes!" Lydia and Archie spoke in unison.

After excusing herself, Patsy returned to the parlor. Before she knew it, Lydia and Archie would be dressed in ball gown and tuxedo. Side by side in his father's surrey.

No doubt, happy memories. Like her own.

"IT'S GONE!" LYDIA STEPPED OUT OF HER bedchamber.

Patsy scooped another chicken bone from the pot on the stove. "What's gone?"

"Gram's trunk!"

Patsy dropped the spoon into the pan. "It can't be."

"You've discovered my surprise?" Mother stood in the doorway.

"Your surprise?" Lydia's eyes had grown to the size of Miss Hattie's tea saucers.

"Yes." Mother faced Lydia. "You will no longer have to trip over my trunk."

"She won't?" Patsy's hand settled on her collar. "You moved the trunk into your bedchamber? There was no room. Besides, it is too heavy for you to be toting."

Mother raised her hand. "The trunk is not in my bedchamber. And I never said I lifted a finger. That nice young man, Archie, took it."

"Archie took it?" Lydia's voice had risen an octave.

Patsy's heart pounded. They'd stitched all but two of the blocks and expected to start piecing them together this very evening. "Where did he take it?"

"It's nothing to get excited about, dear. Old clothes I thought I might do something with one day, but…" Mother's voice trailed off.

Patsy's gaze collided with Lydia's.

"Truth is, I was never going to do anything with them, and it was time to let them go. I saw Archie Saturday when I returned from the luncheon and asked him if he'd mind taking the trunk away for me."

"So he took it this afternoon while I was at the mercantile?"

"That was the best time if I was going to surprise you."

"You did. Thank you for your thoughtfulness." Patsy untied the apron at her waist and tucked stray hairs behind her ear. "I need to go out for a moment. Mother, could you make the dumplings or heat some canned peas?"

"You're going out again?" Mother took the apron from her.

"I'll be home before you have the dumplings ready for the pot." Patsy pulled her scarf and cape from the hat rack in the entryway and dashed out the door. Thankfully, the snowflakes had ceased their drifting earlier in the day. With every step toward the road, her feet sank into a blanket of crunchy snow. Boots would have been favorable over black satin day slippers, but there had been no time.

Her steps swift but careful, Patsy made her way across Golden Avenue and down Third Street, past the new Sisters of Mercy Hospital, then turned left on Bennett Avenue. Archie had to be at the post office with the trunk. They couldn't have lost all the work they'd done. Shaking her head against the distress threatening to topple her, Patsy crossed Bennett

Avenue and stepped onto the wooden boardwalk in front of the post office.

"Mrs. Michaels?"

"Archie!" Patsy spun so fast her head began to swim.

"You don't look like you're feeling well." Gripping her elbow, he guided her toward the bench near the door.

She perched on the edge of the seat. "I rushed down here when I found out what Mother had done. Where did you take the trunk?"

"The parsonage." Archie moistened his lips. "About an hour ago. Your mother told me to find someone who would make good use of the fabric in it."

Her nod exaggerated, Patsy stood. "Good. Please excuse me." She fluttered her hand and turned in the direction of the First Congregational Church.

IN THE FLICKERING LIGHT FROM TWO LANTERNS, Patsy studied the layout of Lydia's bedchamber. The two of them had changed the configuration to make allowance for hiding the trunk in the corner, on the far end of Lydia's wardrobe. The bed now occupied the opposite side of the room.

She'd returned before Warren made it home from work, but not before Mother had posed a series of questions concerning her sudden exit. Passing over any inquiry to do with the disappearing trunk, Patsy talked of her need to speak with Ida Sinclair Tucker at the parsonage.

Lydia gave a crate a nudge. "Reverend Tucker should be able to slide the trunk into this corner, with Gram none the wiser."

"This quilt is proving to be a difficult secret to keep. I didn't expect to say this—not this year, but I'm glad Christmas is only twelve days away."

"And only ten days until the Christmas ball!" Lydia rose up onto her toes. "Vivian said that Friday, while I'm at the shop, I can alter an emerald gown someone brought in for exchange. I'll only have to pay for the dry cleaning after the ball. Plus, I found out that Archie's favorite color is green. I can scarcely wait!"

A nod was all Patsy could manage.

The sound of wagon wheels grinding the frigid road silenced them. Patsy took quiet steps to the front door, glancing up at the empty staircase on her way by. Thankfully, Mother would have drifted off to sleep by now.

WITHIN TWENTY MINUTES, PATSY, LYDIA, AND Ruth were settled into their preferred nests in the parlor, the Nine Patch blocks scattered among them.

"Archie really had to take your elbow and help you to the bench?"

Patsy nodded. "I probably would've landed in a heap on the boardwalk if he hadn't."

"What was that?" Ruth stared at the parlor door.

Patsy hadn't heard anything, but stilled her needle and listened. The stairs creaked. Someone was on their way down. Pressing her finger to her lips, Patsy took quiet steps to the closed door.

Mother stood at the bottom of the staircase, staring at her.

"Is something the matter?"

"I'll say it is. I dreamed someone snuck into the house and stole all the furniture. Seemed so real that I heard scraping on the floor down here. Is everything all right?"

"As far as I know, it is." Patsy cupped Mother's elbow. "And your dream doesn't sound like anything a cup of tea can't dispel."

Making no move toward the kitchen, Mother glanced toward the parlor. "Where is everyone?"

"Joseph is fast asleep. I was sewing. And Warren is in his study reading *A Christmas Carol* for his book club." She needed to steer Mother away from the parlor. "Do you feel like a refreshing peppermint tea? Or a mellow chamomile?"

Thirty minutes later, after watching Mother close the door to her upstairs bedchamber, Patsy returned to the parlor. One look at each other and she, Lydia, and Ruth collapsed on the sofa in a mound of muffled giggles.

Another sweet memory.

PATSY AWOKE TO THE SOUND OF CLATTERING dishes. She yawned. Blinking, she forced her bleary eyes to focus on the clock atop her bureau. Five twenty-five. Warren's soft snore never skipped a beat. Both girls were up especially late last night. Neither of them would choose to be up this early on a Saturday morning. And although Mother had been of more help in the kitchen the last several days, she was too fond of her rocker first thing in the morning to be out and about. Another yawn, and she pulled the Daisy Chain quilt tight at her neck.

Sleep tugged at her until she heard metal on metal. Patsy pulled her dressing gown from a hook on the wall. Her feet halted just outside the kitchen doorway. The room smelled of cinnamon and cloves. Glass bowls flanked her big metal bowl on the cupboard and baking sheets lined the kitchen table. "Mother?"

Mother spun to face her, with a doughy smudge on her cheek. "Good morning, dear."

"What are you doing?"

"I always make my Gold Ore cookies two days before Christmas."

"But—"

"You thought sorrow sickness would keep me from baking my cookies."

"It did seem to be getting—"

"The best of me?"

Patsy nodded.

"Yes, well, the Good Lord and I have been talking about that. Nothing lit by lightning, mind you. But He did speak to me through Scripture. 'A merry heart—'"

"'—doeth good like a medicine.'" Patsy joined Mother in reciting the last of the verse.

"The same Proverb surfaced for me and the girls two weeks ago." Recalling Ruth's *good memories* insertion, Patsy had to smile.

Mother dumped candied currants into the metal bowl, then looked up at Patsy, her brown eyes glistening. "The Lord works in mysterious ways, doesn't He?"

"Yes. He certainly does." *Mysterious and wonderful ways.*

THE ORANGE FLAMES DANCING IN THE FIREPLACE coupled with soft lamplight to cast a glow on the memory-rich cross pattern in the center of a Nine Patch block. Patsy sat on one end of the parlor sofa, and Ruth at the other. Both turned the light-blue floral backing to the front on their respective ends of the quilt. Pulling her needle through the edging, Patsy glanced at Ruth and returned her daughter's smile. Both girls were proving to be proficient seamstresses, but this evening Lydia was otherwise occupied.

Mother's Christmas cookies had never tasted better than they had today. With that, and seeing Archie standing at the foot of the staircase while Lydia beamed wearing the silk gown, and visiting with Ruth over needle and thread, Patsy felt better than she had in several months.

"We'll have Gram's quilt finished within the hour." Regret tinged Ruth's statement.

"It has been fun, hasn't it?"

"I'll miss the evenings working together. You, me, and Lydia. Remembering." Ruth caressed a patch piece from Pop's striped shirt. "You've been...well, I think doing this for Gram has made you feel better too."

"Making the quilt slowed me down long enough to shed a few tears over losing Pop, but it also gave me something productive to do with my grief."

"Me too." Ruth returned her needle to the binding. "It's been good to remember Pop and the life he lived with Gram, while doing something special for her."

"A good reminder too. It's most important that we spend time with those we love."

"Making good memories." Smiling, Ruth shifted her corner of the quilt to stitch the next section. "God comforts us when we're doing something to comfort others."

"It's true." Another good reminder.

She and Ruth spent the next few minutes stitching in a comfortable silence. Until the sound of hooves raised Patsy's head. According to the mantel clock, Archie had five minutes to walk Lydia to the door to meet the ten o'clock curfew. Sticking her needle into the edging, Patsy set her end of the quilt on the sofa and took soft steps to the window.

"Are they here?"

Patsy nodded. Placing her hand on the windowsill for a brace, she bent down at the corner.

"Mama!"

Patsy turned, placing a finger on her lips.

"You're going to peek at them?"

"I shouldn't, I know. But…" Patsy gingerly pulled back the curtain while envisioning Warren doing the same at a corner of the window in the study.

Almost instantly, Ruth crouched at Patsy's side, peering out the window. They watched as Lydia walked toward the house looking like a princess in the emerald gown with the striped black velvet ribbons on the bodice and skirt. Her gloved hand rested on Archie's arm, and Mother's pearls draped her neck. No, Lydia wasn't a little girl anymore. And neither was Ruth.

Patsy sighed, wistful but content. Tonight, she was gathering more memories for her heart to treasure. Certainly, for her and her family, this would be a Christmas far different than any before it. One laced with sadness, yes, but wonderful in so many ways.

And tomorrow night, Mother would behold her surprise.

TRUE TO TRADITION, THE MICHAELS FAMILY, now including Mother, gathered around the tree on the eve before Christmas. Each of them had chosen a favorite carol for the family to sing before opening gifts. "O come, all ye faithful, joyful and triumphant"—the familiar words lingered in Patsy's head. The carol had been her favorite since she was a girl and first heard Pop sing the bass notes on "adore Him, Christ the Lord." Ruth chose "Silent Night"; Joseph, "Away in a Manger." Warren and Lydia shared the same favorite, "Joy to the World," while Mother favored "What Child Is This?"

Warren's fiddle and Joseph's guitar now lay silent on the edge of the velvet tree skirt. Each family member had unwrapped their gifts. New journals topped Lydia and Ruth's stack. Patsy wore the cameo pendant she'd received from Warren. Joseph wore the new cap Gram knit for him.

Wearing a black skirt and a silk red shirtwaist, Mother sat in the wingback chair with the white birdhouse Warren had made for her nestled on her lap. She quietly pressed a scallop-edged handkerchief to her cheek.

Mother had one more gift to unwrap. Patsy started to move, ready to retrieve it from Warren's study, but second thoughts kept her seated. Should she wait until Mother had more time?

Before Patsy could alert the girls to her concern, Ruth disappeared and returned to the parlor, the last gift hidden in a special pillowcase Lydia had made.

"Gram, we have one more present for you." Ruth took quick steps to the wingback.

"Another? But you've already given me so much." She dabbed her eyes with the handkerchief. Lydia took the birdhouse from Mother while Ruth handed her the package.

Joseph was quick to grab the corners of the pillowcase. "You grab what's inside and pull." She did, and he landed on the floor in a pile of giggles.

The quilt unfolded and draped Mother's lap. Her breath caught and her eyes sparkled with what Patsy hoped were tears of joy. "The old clothes!" Mother's crooked fingers trailed the cross pieces in the center block. "Walter's denims. He fairly wore them out working beside me in the garden." Lifting the corner of the quilt to her face, she drew in a long breath.

Tears of joy welled Patsy's eyes. The good memories—the shared memories—didn't erase the loss of Pop or the sting of sorrow, but they had softened the scar on her heart, and would do the same for Mother.

Mother looked at Ruth, who knelt beside Gram's chair, her brown eyes glistening. "How?"

"Mama, Lydia, and I made it."

Joseph sat at his grandmother's feet. "Father's and my big job was to stay out of their way."

Mother looked at Patsy. "You did the sewing in the parlor after I'd gone to bed, didn't you?"

"Yes. And when Miss Hattie took you to the ladies' luncheon."

"But the clothes...that's where you disappeared to after I told you I had them removed, isn't it?"

Nodding, Patsy knelt next to Mother. "Archie had taken the trunk to the parsonage. Reverend Tucker returned it to us that night."

Mother's hand trailed the blocks, stopping on the middle one. "Your pop wore that yellow shirt on our wedding day." A sigh lifted a gray curl from her forehead. Lowering the quilt, her weathered hand caressing its patches, Mother looked at each family member. "What a miraculous Christmas present. You brought him back to me!"

Patsy let her own tears of joy flow. *Thank You, Lord!*

SPECIAL DELIVERY
Susan Page Davis

Maine, December 1913

Ruth Parker pulled the collar of her wool coat higher against the wind and caught her nephew's hand. December was always cold in Maine, but this year was extreme. A week remained until Christmas, but they'd already had eight days of subzero temperatures.

She pulled open the heavy door of the railroad station and all but shoved Benjy inside to escape the bitter cold. The seven-year-old stumbled over the step and stood blinking in the dimness inside.

"Over there." Ruth nodded toward the ticket window.

The man behind the barred window smiled at her. "Hello, Mrs. Parker. How may I help you this morning?"

"I'd like to send my nephew to visit my folks in Bangor over Christmas. That is... if it's not too expensive." Ruth gritted her teeth. She had only a dollar and twenty cents. She and Tim had tried to save up enough for the boy to go and visit his grandparents, but it was hard to put aside anything with their own three little ones and Benjy to feed.

The ticket agent peered over the shelf that separated them and down at Benjy. "Round trip?"

Ruth nodded.

"And a ticket for yourself?"

"No, just Benjamin."

"That will be two dollars and fifty cents."

Ruth gulped. "Isn't there a special rate for children?"

"He's too big to hold on your lap, even if you were going," the agent said.

"Oh. How much is a one-way ticket?"

"A dollar twenty-five."

She sighed. Five cents was all she lacked, but it might as well have been a fortune. She knew her parents wouldn't have the extra money when the time came to send Benjy back to her.

BENJY LOOKED ALL AROUND AT THE INSIDE OF the railroad depot. He'd only been in this place once before, and then only for a few minutes. Lots of signs hung about the room. One pictured a slice of juicy apple pie on a blue plate. It said, "Duncan's Café: The Best Food in Town." He doubted that. Aunt Ruth made the best food in any town.

Another sign hung beside a window like the one where Aunt Ruth stood. He squinted at it and tried to sound out the words. "Parcel Post, New Rates. Average a Penny a Pound." He wondered what that meant.

He was getting warm, so he pulled off his red wool mittens and let them hang from the string around his neck. Next he yanked off his knit hat and shoved it into his pocket.

Aunt Ruth turned away from the window. "Come on, Benjy. Where's your hat? It's cold out. You didn't lose it, did you?"

Benjy pulled the red-and-white hat from his pocket.

"Oh, good. Put it on now. We're going home."

"I want to see Sadie and Frannie. You said I could ride the train to Grandpa Brown's today."

"I know." Aunt Ruth leaned over him with a sigh and pulled his hat down snugly over his ears. "I'm sorry, honey. You can't go today. Now, put your mittens back on."

AT SUPPER THAT NIGHT, UNCLE TIM LOOKED across the table at Benjy and made a funny face, as though he was shocked to see his nephew sitting there in his usual place. Benjy liked Uncle Tim, and he smiled back at him.

"You're still here!" Uncle Tim said. "I thought you were going to Bangor today."

"The tickets cost more than we thought," Aunt Ruth said.

"How much?"

"Two-fifty for the round trip."

"I thought kids were half price."

"Apparently not, if they're going by themselves."

"*Hmm.*" Uncle Tim frowned. Benjy knew it wasn't because Uncle Tim didn't want him there. They were good friends, and Benjy tried to help out with chores. He'd stacked firewood in the cellar last fall, and he always emptied the trash and brought in the bottles of milk every morning.

"I didn't even have quite enough for a one-way." Aunt Ruth passed Uncle Tim the dish of potatoes. The baby, Billy, began to fuss, and she took a slice of carrot off her plate and mashed it on his high chair tray. "Hush, now." The two little girls both nibbled on their biscuits. "Eat your vegetables, girls," Aunt Ruth told them.

"Do you think your folks could pay his way back if we sent him?" Uncle Tim asked.

Aunt Ruth sighed. "I doubt it. I don't think we should ask them."

Benjy watched them, looking back and forth between them. They knew how much he wanted to see his sisters. He liked living here, and after six months, it felt like home. He missed his mom and dad a lot. They were in heaven now, and he couldn't see them again on this earth. But Christmas wouldn't seem right if he couldn't spend it with Sadie and Frannie, his older sisters. Uncle Tim and Aunt Ruth wouldn't mind keeping him over the holidays. They would probably even get him some kind of present, if it didn't cost too much. But he wanted to be with his grandparents and his sisters. Tears stung his eyes, and he blinked them away. He didn't feel much like eating.

"There was a sign that said a penny a pound," he ventured.

Uncle Tim looked at him keenly. "What's that, Benjy?"

"A penny a pound. That's what it said. I don't weigh two hundred pounds."

Aunt Ruth chuckled. "That was for mail, honey. Packages. Not people."

"Put Benjy in a package," his cousin Lucy said with a laugh.

Uncle Tim's eyes twinkled. "What do you think of that, Benjy? We could tie you up in brown paper and twine."

"I don't mind," Benjy said.

"Naw, I was just kidding." His uncle took a big bite of biscuit.

"Benjy's a package," Lucy chanted. She was five, and sometimes she was a pest. Benjy wanted to stick out his tongue at her, but Aunt Ruth wouldn't like that.

"Well, Lucy's a monkey," he muttered.

"Mama! Benjy called me a monkey!" Lucy tugged on her mother's sleeve.

"Monkey," said three-year-old Emily from her chair beside Benjy.

"Hush, Lucy. Eat your supper. You too, Emily. Benjy knows he can't go through the mail like a box of crackers, and he knows you're a girl, not a monkey, so be quiet."

"I wouldn't mind," Benjy said again.

"You'd be scared in a package," Lucy insisted.

"No, I wouldn't. I'd just sleep the whole way to Bangor."

"Well, I'd be scared," she said, her blue eyes wide.

"You're a baby."

"Benjy, that's enough," Aunt Ruth said in her no-nonsense voice.

Benjy ducked his head. He didn't like it when Aunt Ruth got upset with him. She mostly did it when he fought with Lucy. He tried not to, but sometimes Lucy pushed him too far.

"I'm sorry," he mumbled.

"I wonder..." Uncle Tim sat with his forkful of carrots halfway to his mouth, staring at the wall above Benjy's head.

"Wonder what?" Aunt Ruth asked.

"If they really could take him as freight. He can't weigh more than fifty or sixty pounds."

Aunt Ruth frowned. "You're joking, right?"

"Oh, I don't mean we'd stuff him in a box, but why couldn't we pay freight prices?"

"Would they stick him in a freight car?"

Uncle Tim shrugged. "I don't know. I guess we can ask Harry Locke. He handles the mail car between here and Bangor. And it's only sixty miles." He smiled at Benjy. "You wouldn't be scared, would you?"

Benjy shook his head, though he wasn't really sure. He didn't know this man, Harry, but if he was a friend of Uncle Tim's, it would probably be all right.

"Tell you what," Uncle Tim said. "I'll take Benjy to the station tomorrow morning early, when they're sorting the mail, and we'll see what Harry says about it."

Benjy began to eat then. His stomachache had vanished. Maybe he would get to spend Christmas with his sisters and grandparents after all.

"CAN'T DO IT," HARRY SAID THE NEXT MORNING.

"Why not?" Uncle Tim walked beside him as Harry pushed a dolly carrying three mail sacks across the railroad platform, and Benjy tagged along. He wasn't going to lose sight of his uncle in this busy place.

Harry paused and looked around. "My boss is kind of finicky."

"Well, if there's a rule against it..."

Harry sighed. "I'm not sure if there is one or not. People can't go as freight, Tim. I know that. As for parcel post...that system is all new. If there is a rule, and Mr. Darrow heard I'd broken it... Well, you can see that it puts me in a spot." Harry was taller than Uncle Tim, and Benjy had to look way up high to see his scowl. Harry had a face like rubber, and right now it was lined with frowny wrinkles. "I don't want to risk my job."

"I wouldn't want you to do that," Uncle Tim assured him. "Do you have a list of what you can accept and what you can't? I'm sure you're not allowed to take explosives, for instance."

"You got that right," Harry said. "Stuff like dynamite can go as freight, but not on passenger trains, and you have to have special permission."

"So can we take a look at the list?"

Harry pulled out his watch and looked at it, then shoved it back in his pocket. "We've got fifteen minutes until the train comes, and I have to get on it with these sacks of mail." He hesitated a moment, then sighed and turned back toward the depot, pushing the dolly. "Come on. I can't leave the mail sitting on the platform. Mr. Darrow would fire me for sure if I did that."

Inside the station, Harry went behind the counter. Benjy couldn't see him, but Uncle Tim craned his neck, looking through one of the barred windows in the wall. Soon Harry came out carrying an open booklet with a green cover.

"I can't find anything clearly against it, but I'm sure this new program wasn't meant for people. I mean, if folks heard about it, they'd be appalled."

"It's not like we'd bundle him up in a box," Uncle Tim said. "I thought he could ride with you in the mail car."

Harry shook his head, his eyes not focused on anything. "Mr. Darrow comes here at least once a week, just to make sure we're all on the job. He hasn't been here since last Monday, and everyone's on edge, thinking he'll pop up any minute."

"But if the regulations don't say anything against it—"

Harry looked around anxiously. "Let's go over there." He pulled the dolly into a corner of the room, out of the way of passengers and people who had come to ship packages. Benjy scuttled behind Uncle Tim and held on to his pant leg. Harry looked fretfully toward the door leading out to the platform.

"He misses his sisters a lot," Uncle Tim said. "We took Benjy in after his folks died, but we couldn't take all three kids. Ruth's parents have kept the girls, and Benjy needs to see them now and again."

Harry thumbed through the manual's pages. "Here's the list of items we can't accept."

Benjy watched his uncle's face while he studied the booklet. He frowned, but then his expression cleared, and he looked up.

"Not one word about children."

"But—"

"Ruth said Nelly Merritt got the postman to carry her baby in his bag all the way across town to her mother a couple of weeks ago."

"But she wasn't mailing him."

"Well, no, and the postman's her cousin."

"It's not the same. This is a railroad, Tim. It's a good job, and I don't want to lose it."

"No one will know," Uncle Tim said. "You do the weighing and write up the order, or whatever it is you'd do with a package."

Harry looked toward the ticket window and the postal counter. "Speaking of which, someone's waiting for service. I've got to help her."

He hurried behind the counter, taking the rulebook with him.

"Come on, Benjy." Uncle Tim took his hand firmly. Benjy thought he was going to lead him out into the cold and take him home, but to his surprise, they walked over to the postal window and got in line behind the woman Harry was assisting.

"That'll be thirty-five cents." Harry took the lady's package and put it down behind the counter. The woman gave him some coins.

"Thank you," she said and turned away.

Uncle Tim stepped up to the window. "I have a parcel to ship to Bangor." He stooped and hefted Benjy up to sit on the counter.

Harry frowned at them through the bars. After a long moment, he said gruffly, "Bring it outside."

On the platform, he led them to a scale. "We weigh luggage here, Benjy. Hop on."

Benjy stepped cautiously onto the small platform. Uncle Tim placed his small bag of extra clothing in his hand. Harry looked at the scale. "That's too much. There's a fifty-pound limit."

Uncle Tim took back the bag of clothes.

"That just does it." Harry scribbled on the top sheet of his pad. "Follow me."

Back inside the depot, Harry filled out a cardboard ticket with a hole punched in it. He threaded a piece of twine through the hole and draped it around Benjy's neck.

"There's a base rate, plus a per-pound charge. That's fifty-eight cents all told." Again, Harry peered around the room. "Hurry."

Uncle Tim counted out the coins. A woman came and stood behind them at the window.

"Wait on the platform," Harry said.

The woman stepped up and placed a small box on the counter. Uncle Tim grabbed Benjy's hand and hustled him outside. In the distance the train's whistle blew. Benjy's heart thumped in his chest. He had never ridden a train before. He squeezed Uncle Tim's hand hard.

Uncle Tim crouched beside him and put a hand on Benjy's back. "You'll be fine. Grandma will find you something to wear. Just do whatever Harry tells you on the train."

"He won't put me in a box?"

"No, he won't." Uncle Tim smiled and touched the tag that hung around Benjy's neck. "This is your ticket. Now, don't forget to mind Grandpa and Grandma. And next week, you'll ride back to us."

Benjy nodded. Tears blurred his view of Uncle Tim's face.

"Hey, Benjy, it's going to be all right. Pretty soon you'll be playing with Sadie and Frannie." Uncle Tim took several coins out of his pocket. "Put these in your mitten and give them to Grandpa when you get there. He can use it toward your return ticket next week."

Benjy pulled out the cuff of his left mitten, and Uncle Tim slid the coins in, one by one. What if Grandpa didn't have enough extra to send him back?

The whistle blew again, louder, and the train whooshed into the station. Benjy clapped his hands over his ears and braced against the fierce wind the locomotive made as it screeched to a halt. Suddenly, Harry was bending over him, patting his chest. Benjy looked down. Harry was sticking postage stamps to the front of his coat.

"All right, come with me." Harry jerked his head and started pushing the dolly of mail sacks toward the third car of the train.

Uncle Tim gave Benjy a quick hug. "Go on, now. I'll see you next week."

Benjy ran to catch up with Harry. He didn't want to be left behind now!

Harry hauled open the door to the mail car and tossed the three sacks inside. Beside the door, fixed to the outside of the car, was a long arm with a hook on the end. Benjy wondered what it was for.

Harry turned and looked around the platform, then said to Benjy, "In you go."

Benjy stepped into the long railroad car. Boxes and sacks were lined up along one side, and across from them was a long row of canvas bins. On the wall hung a rack divided into pigeonholes, and a small stove sat near one end. Harry gently pushed him farther in.

"Step to the side here, away from the door, so people outside can't see you. You can sit on that box."

Benjy sat down and huddled on the box with his hands in his coat pockets. The coins in his mitten were starting to warm up from the heat of his fingers.

"I'll be right back." Harry went out and rolled the big door shut.

Inside the car, it was dark. Benjy tried to breathe slowly and steadily, but he felt like crying. It was cold in here. The lumpy mail sacks were weird, pale humps. What if one of them was a monster? He shivered and wondered if Harry would really come back, and if he would really get to Bangor safely. Lucy had been right—he was scared, even if he wasn't in a box. He hated knowing she'd been right.

The door rolled open, and light flooded in, along with Harry. He didn't say anything, but set a notebook and pencil in one of the pigeonholes and lit two lanterns that hung from brackets on the ceiling. He closed the door and looked over at Benjy.

"We'll be pulling out any minute now."

Once the train began to chug and move over the rails, Harry seemed to relax. He grinned at Benjy. "Hey, pal, how would you like to help me sort some letters?"

Benjy swallowed hard. "What do I do?"

Harry took a handful of envelopes from a small sack. "These came in this morning, and the postmaster didn't have time to sort them before I loaded the sacks. Let's see, this one's going to Houlton, so we'll put it in this bin here." He held out the letter.

Benjy took off his mittens and let them hang on their string. He took the envelope and stood up. The floor swayed a little beneath his feet, but he could walk slowly as they traveled. He smiled at Harry.

Harry nodded encouragement. "That's it. Just drop it in the bin."

Benjy held the letter over the open canvas bin and let it fall in on top of a pile of other mail.

"Good job," Harry said. He looked at the next one. "This one's for Pittsfield. See that sack yonder? Carry it over there."

Harry walked with him to where several canvas pouches were stacked. He opened one that had twine tied around the middle and "Pittsfield" in black letters on the side. Benjy dropped the letter in.

It took them only minutes to sort the few letters. They both sat down. "Our next stop is Waterville," Harry said. "We pick up passengers there, and I'll get off for the sacks. You just stay put. For Pittsfield and Newport, I'll grab them with my hook."

"What's that?" Benjy asked.

"Did you see the big hook outside the door when we came in?"

Benjy nodded.

"I flip a lever, and it flies out to grab the mail pouch off a crane on the station platform. You'll see."

Benjy smiled. So that was what the hook was for. Harry grabbed things with it. Did he ever grab people by mistake? Benjy was glad he'd been mailed from a station where the train stopped every day, instead of one that hung its sacks out to be grabbed.

The braking train made a whooshing, screeching sound, and Harry stood up. "We're coming up on Waterville." He grabbed a bar that was screwed to the wall and hung on as the train slowed and stopped. Benjy braced himself with his feet so he wouldn't fall off his box.

A door at the far end of the mail car opened, and a man walked in. Benjy's heart pounded, and he curled low on the box. He'd had no idea there was another door to this railroad car. Did Harry know?

"Hey, Harry!" The newcomer advanced down the car. He wore a blue overcoat with shiny buttons. His hat had a gleaming medal on the front, and a silver whistle hung from a cord clipped to his shoulder.

"What's up, Joe?" Harry asked.

"Did you hear? Mr. Darrow's boarding here. He's riding along to Bangor."

Harry's face looked odd. "Is he going to inspect the train?"

"Don't know," Joe said. "It wouldn't surprise me." His gaze lit on Benjy. "Ho! What's this?"

"Just some parcel post we picked up in Oakland."

"You don't say." Joe reached out and turned Benjy's tag upward and perused it. "Looks official."

"Yes, and paid for too."

Joe eyed the stamps and laughed.

"But I don't care to have Mr. Darrow seeing him," Harry added, rolling the big door open.

Joe frowned. "Is it regulation?"

"I couldn't find anything against it." Harry caught his breath. "There he is!"

Joe went over to the door and looked out with Harry. Benjy tried to squeeze himself even smaller.

"Morning, sir," he heard Harry yell.

"I'll come by to see you later," a faint voice replied.

After a moment, Harry said, "Whew. I'd better get these sacks off while he's getting settled up front."

"Yes, and I'd best get back to the passenger car," Joe said. "I'll try to alert you when he starts to make the rounds." He smiled at Benjy. "Have a good trip, young fellow."

Joe went back the way he came, and Harry said, "I'll just be a minute here, Benjy. You keep your head down."

Benjy watched him leave, afraid to move. It seemed to him that Harry was gone a long time. Finally a shadow blocked most of the doorway, and a dolly loaded with sacks came in, followed by Harry, who was pushing it. Benjy let out a big sigh.

Harry grinned at him. "All right, pard?"

Benjy nodded.

A few minutes later, they were rolling again, with the cars rumbling and rattling over the tracks. Harry sorted a bag full of letters and packages into bins and sacks and then turned to Benjy.

"Next station, we'll just roll through, and we'll snatch the pouch of mail with the hook." He picked up one of the mail pouches. "I have to kick their sack of letters out the door right when we grab their outgoing mail. You can watch, but stay back, out of the way."

Fascinated, Benjy sat where Harry told him and watched him open the door partway. Harry placed the heavy canvas bag of mail for Pittsfield on the floor in front of the door and put his hand on a lever on the wall beside it. Outside, trees and houses rushed by. The train whistled, and suddenly Harry flipped the lever. A sack of mail flew in through the doorway, and Benjy jumped. He was glad he'd kept back, like Harry told him. Almost at the same time the pouch landed on the floor, Harry kicked out the other sack and shut the door. He turned around and grinned at Benjy.

"You'll catch flies if you sit there with your mouth hanging open."

Benjy closed his mouth, and Harry laughed.

"Come on, pard. We've got more mail to sort."

Harry stooped to open the new mail sack, and they quickly sorted it.

"Newport coming up," Harry said.

Benjy moved to his box and watched him snatch the Newport mail and kick out another sack. He was about to rejoin Harry when the door at the end of the car opened, and Benjy stiffened.

Harry stood straight and waited for the other man, Joe, to come closer.

"The boss is on the prowl," Joe said. "He'll be here in a minute."

Harry whirled and pulled a large canvas sack out of a bin. "Come on, Benjy. You're going to pretend you're a parcel, just for a few minutes."

Joe shook his head. "That'll make it worse if he catches you."

"It's worth a try."

Benjy's heart galloped in time with the clacking train wheels as Harry opened the buckle on the bag. "Come on, kid. I promise I won't leave you in there long."

"Want me to stay?" Joe asked.

"Maybe you can help me distract him," Harry said.

Joe looked at his watch. "All right, but if he doesn't come within five minutes, I'll have to get back up front."

"Right." Harry crouched and gestured for Benjy to climb into the mail sack.

Benjy walked over to him slowly, balancing with the movement of the train. He put a hand on Harry's shoulder and moved his feet so that both were in the bottom of the sack. He sucked in a breath and searched Harry's face for reassurance.

"What's the matter, pard?" Harry asked.

"I thought it wasn't against the law for me to ride with you. Will they put us in jail if they find out?"

"No, no." Harry ruffled his hair and glanced toward the far end of the car. "It's not against the law.

My boss is just picky. This is a precaution, to keep him from being upset."

Benjy still wasn't sure it was all right. "Will you get fired?" he asked.

"I hope not. We're just staying on the safe side, pard. Come on, sit down and I'll close the sack and put you in that bin over there." He waved toward an empty bin. "You'll have to be really still. But it won't be for long, and I'll let you out as soon as he's gone."

Benjy gazed at his face for a long moment. He had to trust Harry. Uncle Tim trusted him. He sat down, and Harry pulled the sack up around him. He did something to fasten it shut. Benjy opened his eyes, but he couldn't see anything. Then Harry lifted him. It felt strange to be carried on the swaying car. He was deposited gently in the mail bin, and then he felt something being laid over the part of the sack where his legs were.

"Now, try not to move," Harry said, close to his head.

Far away, Benjy heard Joe call, "Good afternoon, Mr. Darrow!"

A moment later, Harry said, "Hello, sir. Welcome to the mail car."

Benjy's nose itched, but he didn't move his hand to scratch it. He couldn't wiggle, or even breathe hard. He tried to make each breath not move his chest or the sack.

HARRY TRIED NOT TO LOOK AT THE BIN WHERE Benjy's sack rested. He smiled and chatted affably with Mr. Darrow for a moment and hoped he was conveying how smoothly the railroad post office was running.

He inadvertently glanced toward the bin that concealed Benjy. His heart almost stopped as the sacks in it shifted ever so slightly. Mr. Darrow glanced around, but at that moment, Joe went over and leaned on the edge of the bin next to Benjy's, placing his body between it and Mr. Darrow, blocking it from his view.

"Pretty slick operation, eh, sir?"

"Yes." The whistle blew, and Mr. Darrow said, "We're coming up on the Carmel station."

The train started braking. Harry and Mr. Darrow grabbed the wall bar, and Joe braced himself on the sorting rack. The cars ground to a halt, and they adjusted their balance. Mr. Darrow held out his hand to shake Harry's.

"I'd best get back to the passenger car. Thank you, Mr. Locke."

"You're welcome," Harry said.

As Mr. Darrow turned away, a distinct sneeze came from Joe's direction, though it sounded a bit muffled.

Harry and the boss both looked at Joe, who clapped a hand to his nose.

"Sorry," Joe said. He gave an exaggerated sniff.

"Gesundheit." Mr. Darrow nodded at Harry and walked toward the far end of the car.

Joe threw Harry a wide-eyed look and followed Mr. Darrow out through the vestibule door. When the door closed, Harry let out a deep sigh. He hurried over to the bin and unbuckled Benjy's sack.

"You all right, pal?"

Benjy poked his head up. "Yes. But I sneezed. Is he gone?"

"Yeah. He thought it was Joe sneezing. This is our last stop before Bangor. We'll be there in twenty minutes." Benjy's little face looked red and worried. Harry winked at him. "You can get out now. You did great, pard."

"Don't you have to get mail here?"

"Yeah. You want to stay in the bin while I get it?"

"Maybe I'd better."

HARRY RETRIEVED THE CARMEL MAIL IN RECORD time and helped Benjy out of the sack as their journey resumed. When the train pulled in at Bangor, Benjy waited while he unloaded all the mail sacks. Harry whistled as he worked and didn't seem to worry about being discovered now that they had reached their destination.

Finally he came back with a load of new sacks and put them in one of the empty bins. He turned to Benjy. "Come on, pal. There's some people outside who are looking for you. I told them I'd bring you out."

He took Benjy's hand and led him out onto the platform. The air was cold, but the sun was daz-zlingly bright. Benjy squeezed his eyes shut for a moment.

"Benjy!" His sister Frannie hurtled toward him. Sadie wasn't far behind.

Frannie barreled into him so hard that Benjy sat down with a *whoosh*. Sadie laughed and reached out both hands to pull him up. Behind them were Grandpa and Grandma Brown, all wrapped up in coats, scarves, knit hats, and gloves, and smiling so broadly that Benjy was sure they were glad to see him.

"Well, well." Grandpa eyed the tag around Benjy's neck and the stamps on his coat. "I see you have a tale to tell."

Grandma enveloped him in a woolly hug. "Ruth said you might come yesterday, but when you weren't on the train, we thought for sure it would be today. And then you didn't get off today either."

"This young man told us to be patient," Grandpa said, nodding at Harry. "I guess it was worth the wait."

Benjy was bursting to tell them about hiding in the mail bin, but that could wait. Right now he just wanted to get to Grandpa and Grandma's warm house and drink hot cocoa and play with his sisters. He pulled off his left mitten and held out a fistful of coins.

"I have money for you, Grandpa. It's for when I go back to Aunt Ruth and Uncle Tim's house."

"Well, there!" Grandpa smiled as Benjy dropped the coins into his hand.

"Oops, look sharp, pard." Harry snatched the string with the tag off over Benjy's head and tucked it into his pocket. A man in a long overcoat and dark hat was striding toward them.

"This is the railroad's division agent," Harry said to Grandpa. "Hello, Mr. Darrow. This is one of our customers, Mr. Brown, and his family."

"Are you traveling on the rail line?" Mr. Darrow asked.

"No, we just came to pick up something," Grandpa said. "Good service on the mail train."

Mr. Darrow nodded and glanced down at Benjy. Suddenly, Benjy realized the stamps were still stuck to the front of his coat. It was all he could do not to tear them off while Mr. Darrow watched.

"Well, I hope your family enjoys a happy Christmas together," Mr. Darrow said. "Especially now that your package has arrived safely." Benjy was startled to see the stern-looking man give him a wink and a quick smile.

Mr. Darrow turned to Harry and shook his hand. "Merry Christmas, Locke. The postmaster here says your work is outstanding."

"Oh, thank you, sir." Harry face went red. "I'd better get aboard."

"As should I." Mr. Darrow nodded at the family and walked away.

"Good-bye, folks." Harry patted Benjy's shoulder and walked quickly to the mail car. In the doorway, he turned back and waved.

"Good-bye! Merry Christmas!" Benjy waved. A little part of him wished he could ride the train again with Harry. But right now, he was just happy to spend Christmas with his sisters.

THE PLUM PUDDING
PHENOMENON

Kae Noyce Tienstra

Lakeview, Colorado, December 1956

The back door burst open and eleven-year-old Amy Norris, tears streaming down her face, stormed into the kitchen. Cold December air swept in with her as she slammed her books on the counter and tore off her coat and hat.

"Hey, close the door!" piped eight-year-old Rob, who was sitting across the Formica kitchen table from his twin brother Max.

"Yeah! I'm freezing!" echoed Max.

"Oh, Mom, what am I gonna do?" Amy cried, ignoring her brothers and flinging her coat and hat onto a peg by the door. She plopped down on a kitchen chair and buried her head in her arms on the table. Max, grumbling, got up to shut the door.

"Amy, what's wrong?" asked her mother, Abigail, placing a plate of cookies in front of the boys.

"Our family is so boring! Mrs. Anderson told us that we all have to write an essay for a contest!" Amy raised her head, her eyes swollen and red, her hair askew. "We have to write about 'My Family's Christmas Traditions' and why they're special."

"Well, that sounds like fun." Amy's mother soothed her long blonde hair out of her eyes and handed her a tissue.

"Fun?" Amy gave her mother a skeptical look through her tears. "Maybe for *some* of the kids it will be fun. Like Gloria Hansom—oh, she's just *thrilled.* 'Ooh!'" Amy mimicked her classmate, the "queen" of Lakeview Elementary. "'I'll write about our Christmas trip to Aspen. We go every year and ski on Christmas Eve!'

"And Bobby Morton," Amy continued. "His dad decorates their yard every year. Last year it was a North Pole wonderland and it won some kind of award. Bobby said his dad just finished putting up this year's display. It's called 'Christmas Candyland.' That's what Bobby will write about. But what about *me*? Our family doesn't do anything like that." Amy grabbed a cookie from the plate and bit into it fiercely.

"Well, maybe that's okay." Amy's mother poured herself a cup of coffee and sat down next to her children. Both boys ate their cookies, blissfully quiet for once as they munched. "Our family has other ways of celebrating the season. Maybe you can write about those."

Amy couldn't help but roll her eyes. "What? Decorating the Christmas tree? Singing in the church choir? Making popcorn and singing carols on Christmas Eve? Hanging Daddy's big old wool socks by the fireplace?" Max and Rob giggled, and Amy glared at them before looking back at her mother. "Everyone does that! What's special about those things?" She felt her bottom lip quivering.

"Well, that's for *you* to figure out," said her mother. "Every family celebrates Christmas in its own way. And that's what makes their Christmas traditions special. I think your teacher wants you to really think about our Christmas traditions and why they're special to *you*."

Amy thought for a moment. "But, Mom, that's the problem." Her eyes brimmed with tears again. "Our Christmas traditions are boring! Those other kids have cool families who do such amazing things. It'll be easy for Gloria and Bobby to write their essays! But our family is so dull." She glanced at her mother. "I'm sorry, Mom, but we *never* do exciting things like they do. We're just boring and ordinary! And now that

Daddy's lost his job"—she glanced quickly toward her younger brothers and lowered her voice—"I bet we won't even have a Christmas. Bobby and some of his friends laughed at me and said I should write about Christmas traditions when your dad is out of work!"

She stood up, grabbed her books off the counter, and began crying again as she headed for the stairs.

Upstairs in her room Amy threw herself on her bed and let the tears flow. What could she write about? She'd never be able to come up with something interesting for the contest. Amy wondered if her family would even put up a tree.

She thought about last Christmas, when Daddy was the manager of Johnson's Department Store, and the family had been laden with gifts. But then two months later, Johnson's went out of business. Daddy lost his job and couldn't find another one. Now he was installing storm doors just to make enough money to feed the family.

The tears started afresh, and Amy cried herself to sleep.

AMY AWOKE TO THE AROMA OF SLOPPY JOES wafting up from the kitchen.

"Amy, it's time for dinner," her father called.

"I'm coming," Amy mumbled and headed for the stairs.

Her family was already seated at the kitchen table, and Amy took her place across from the boys.

"You look tired, Amybean," said Daddy. "Are you okay?"

"I'm fine," said Amy. "Just sleepy."

He gave her a wink and a smile, but she could see the concern in his eyes.

After dinner the children helped their mother clean up the kitchen, and then Amy and the boys settled in front of the television to watch *I Love Lucy*. Amy's mom and dad lingered at the table talking softly together.

Amy enjoyed Lucys' grape-stomping antics for a few minutes, but she felt too restless to keep watching television. She headed back toward the kitchen for a glass of water but stopped just outside the kitchen door when she heard her parents talking. She waited in the dim hallway, listening.

"I made a bit of money on the Nelson job today," said Daddy, "but not nearly what I expected."

"I'm sorry, Joe," said Mom. "I know how hard you're working."

Amy peeked around the door and saw her father run his hand through his thick black hair. "I'm happy to have a job, really I am," he said. "But installing doors at this time in my life? I'm barely making enough to pay the bills." He sighed. "I don't know what we'll do about Christmas."

"I've told the kids that things are tough," said Mom. "They know not to expect much."

"I hate disappointing them," Amy's father said. He sipped his coffee. "But we've got to cut corners somehow."

"What about a Christmas tree?" asked Amy's mother.

"I think we can manage that. But if we want to give the kids a few presents, I'm afraid plum pudding is out. Those ingredients add up fast at the grocery, especially when you make as much of it as we do."

"Oh no!" Mom's voice rose, then dropped. "Can't we take a bit of money out of savings for the ingredients? *Everyone* counts on plum pudding—it's a family tradition!"

"I know, I know," Daddy said. "But we don't have much left in the savings."

Amy bit her bottom lip. *We always make plum pudding! We* have *to make plum pudding.*

"Maybe we could ask your mother for a small loan to tide us over," Mom suggested.

"I won't do that," said Daddy. "She has her own problems since Dad died."

"Well, we have a few days to figure it out," her mother said. "Maybe we can find some extra dollars somewhere."

Amy heard her father's chair push back as he stood to put his coffee cup in the sink. "Ever the optimist, aren't you?"

Amy darted back through the living room and ran up the stairs before her father saw her. When she got back to her room she sat at her desk and tried to start her homework. She took out her geography book but just couldn't concentrate.

Jumbled thoughts bounced around her mind. Though she knew her parents tried to hide their worries about her father losing his job, she had seen how tired her father was after coming home from his new job.

But Christmas wouldn't be Christmas without plum pudding. Her father loved telling them the story of how his great-great-great-grandfather brought the recipe from England and how the Norrises had made it at Christmas ever since. Amy couldn't remember a Christmas without it.

If there was only something she could do. Maybe she could get a job. *I should talk to Mr. Winslow!* Amy's family always shopped at Winslow's Grocery Store, and Mr. Winslow even sang in the church choir with Mom. *I'll go see Mr. Winslow tomorrow to see if I can help in the store.*

Her decision made, Amy felt much better. She opened her geography book and started her homework.

"Is it okay if I go with Kathy to Winslow's Grocery after school?" Amy asked the next morning. "She needs to pick up something for her mom." Amy figured maybe a tiny white lie would be okay if it was for a good cause.

"All right," said her mother, packing lunches for the boys. "Just be sure you're home by four thirty."

When she got to school Amy sat at her desk in Mrs. Anderson's room and reached for her arithmetic book. Susan Gonzalez, who sat across the aisle, turned to Amy. "Have you started your essay yet?" she whispered, her brown eyes dancing.

Amy panicked. "Why? When are they due?"

"Not till next Monday, December 17," said Susan. She smiled proudly. "I'm writing about how my family celebrated Christmas in Mexico last year."

Mexico! Amy sighed. Everyone seemed to have exciting Christmas traditions but her.

After school Amy walked down Main Street toward Winslow's Grocery. She thought again about the contest. She still had no idea what she would write about, but right now she had more important things on her mind.

When she walked into the store, she found Mr. Winslow arranging oranges in the produce department. "Hi, Mr. Winslow," said Amy.

"Well, hello, young lady." Mr. Winslow paused from his work. "How are you today? Are you picking up something for your mom?"

"No, sir," said Amy. "I came to talk to you."

"To me? Well, what a nice surprise," he said. "Let's just walk back to the bakery. We can talk better there."

Amy followed Mr. Winslow through the produce department and into the fragrant bakery, where Mrs. Winslow was busy putting out colorful Christmas cookies. "Why, hello, Amy! she said. "How nice to see you!"

"Amy and I won't get in your way, Edith," said Mr. Winslow. "We just have to chat for a few minutes." He turned to Amy. "Now, what's on your mind?"

"Plum pudding. Do you remember how we always shop for plum pudding ingredients here at Christmastime?"

"How could I forget?" He smiled. "Plum pudding is quite a tradition for your family. Your folks always give a pudding to Edith and me, and we love it!"

"I love it with lemon sauce on top," added Mrs. Winslow as she placed a chocolate cake on the counter.

Amy grinned. "Yeah, everyone loves it." She felt her smile fade. "But we might not make it this year. Daddy lost his job, and I heard him and my mom saying they don't have much money." She looked at Mr. and

Mrs. Winslow, caught her breath, then continued. "We need a lot of stuff to make plum pudding—a lot! So I had an idea..." Amy looked down at her shoes, uncertain how to say the next part. "So I was wondering," she began again, "if I could work for you here and then maybe you could pay me with all the stuff we need to make plum pudding!"

Mr. Winslow opened his mouth to speak, then looked at his wife before continuing. "So you want to work for me," he said softly. "What a creative girl you are! Plum pudding must mean a whole lot to you."

"Oh, it does! When I heard Mom and Dad saying we might not make it this year"—tears stung Amy's eyes—"that's when I thought about you and the store." She quickly dried her eyes on her sleeve and took another deep breath. "I could sweep the floors, or help here in the bakery, or even learn the cash register. I'm real good with people; I could bag groceries or maybe stock the shelves!"

"Oh, honey, you're pretty young for all that," said Mrs. Winslow.

Amy bowed her head, afraid she might start to cry again. She didn't want to cry in front of the Winslows.

Mrs. Winslow came around to the front of the counter and whispered in her husband's ear. Mr. Winslow grinned. "Good idea, Edith!"

The Winslows turned to Amy, both of them smiling ear to ear. "Amy, my wife and I have another idea—one that could help all of us!" said Mr. Winslow.

"Why don't you just sit down for a moment and eat this donut," said Mrs. Winslow, "while we tell you what we have in mind?"

Amy left the store several minutes later with powdered sugar on her lips and wings on her feet.

ABIGAIL NORRIS WAS CLEANING UP THE KITCHEN the next day when the phone rang.

"Good morning, Abigail. This is Henry Winslow."

"Henry, so nice to hear from you. How are you?"

"Well, I'm just fine, Abigail. I'm calling you with a rather unusual Christmas proposition."

"Oh?" laughed Abigail. "What's up?"

"A plum pudding party," said Henry. "I saw Amy in the store yesterday and she reminded me that plum pudding season is here. You know how Edith and I always enjoy the pudding you give us."

"I'm glad you enjoy it, Henry," said Abigail, "but—"

"Now, you may think this is an unusual request, but I was wondering if you'd be willing to teach Edith and me how you make it."

"You want to learn how to make plum pudding?" asked Abigail, laughing again. "It's sort of a family secret, you know."

"We'll never tell a soul." Henry chuckled. "You know we love the stuff—we ate that pudding you gave us last year in one sitting! Here's my idea: you give me a list of the ingredients you need, and Edith and I will bring them from the store to your house— our treat. Then we can help you make plum pudding, and you and Joe can teach us your secrets in the process. Edith and I would love to make it ourselves and maybe offer it to some of our customers next Christmas."

"Well, I'm speechless," said Abigail. "It's odd. Joe and I were just discussing plum pudding, and, well, let's just say your offer couldn't have come at a better time! You know Joe lost his job?"

"Yes, I know Johnson's closed."

Abigail was quiet for a moment. "Wait a minute— you're not doing this just to help us out, I hope?"

"You'd be doing us a favor by sharing your recipe and teaching us how to make it. The least we can do is to supply the ingredients! So what do you say? Could you put up with Edith and me in your kitchen?"

"Of course we could! I'll need to talk to Joe, but I'm sure he'd be thrilled. Let's do it! We always make plum pudding at least a week before Christmas to give it time to age a bit. How does this Saturday sound?"

Abigail heard Henry rifling through his calendar. "The fifteenth? Sounds good to me. What time?"

"Let's say ten o'clock."

"It's a date," said Henry. "If you put together a list of the ingredients you need, I'll stop by tonight and pick it up."

"I'll be here," said Abigail. "And you can run your idea by Joe when you come. Thank you so much for thinking of this, Henry—this will be such fun!"

LATER THAT AFTERNOON JOE NORRIS WAS PUTTING his tools away for the day. He'd just finished a difficult door installation at the O'Haras' house, just a few blocks from home.

Mrs. O'Hara called to him from the kitchen. "Joe, phone for you. It's Dr. Kellogg."

Joe's heart skipped a beat as he took the receiver.

"Joe, I'm sorry to call you on the job," said Dr. Kellogg. "Abigail had a little accident this afternoon."

"Abigail? Is she all right?"

"She's just fine, Joe. She had a little fall. She's here in my office with one heck of a cast on her arm. Your mom brought her here after the accident, but she had to go right back to your house to wait for the kids. Can you come pick Abigail up?"

Joe felt his legs get wobbly and he sat in the chair Mrs. O'Hara offered. "But how? What did she—?"

"Here, Joe, I'll let Abigail explain," said Dr. Kellogg.

Joe breathed a sigh of relief when he heard Abigail's voice on the line. "Oh, Joe, I'm so sorry. It was just a stupid accident! I was taking a load of dirty clothes down the stairs and I stepped wrong, fell, and broke my arm!"

Joe could hear that Abigail was near tears. "It's okay, honey, I'll be right there."

He drove as quickly as he could to Dr. Kellogg's office. Abigail was sitting in the waiting room when he arrived. She looked pale and scared with a big white plaster cast on her right arm. She stood and Joe gingerly took her into his arms. After a few moments he stepped back to look more closely at her. "So you're all right?"

"I'm fine," said Abigail, as Dr. Kellogg came into the waiting room. "I'm just embarrassed."

"Hi, Joe, hope I didn't scare you too bad," said Dr. Kellogg. He looked at Abigail. "You've got a tough wife. The break isn't too bad, but she should rest for the next week and not use her right hand at all. Bring her back in a few days and we'll see how she's doing."

AMY KNEW SOMETHING WAS WRONG THE MINUTE she opened the kitchen door. Mom was not in the kitchen and the boys were nowhere to be seen. Daddy was talking on the phone and he signaled to Amy to go into the living room.

"Mom?" called Amy.

"We're in here, Amy." Grandma Louise's voice came from the living room.

"Grandma, what are you..."

There on the couch sat her mother, a twin on each side of her. She smiled weakly at Amy and held up her right arm.

"Mom, what happened?" asked Amy, rushing to kneel in front of her mother.

Mom explained how she broke her arm and assured Amy and the boys that she'd be up and about in no time. "Doctor K just wants me to take it easy for a few days."

Amy's father came in from the kitchen, wiping his hands on a dish towel. "That was Henry Winslow on the phone. He said he's on his way over. Do you know what he wants?"

"Oh!" Amy's mother cried. "I forgot all about Henry!" She sat up straight on the sofa. "Joe, I didn't have a chance to tell you after the accident, but this morning Henry called to ask if he and Edith could help us make plum pudding. They want to learn how to do it, and Henry said they'd supply all the ingredients— his treat. But look at me! I can't even make a cup of coffee, let alone plum pudding!"

Amy couldn't believe it. Mr. Winslow *had* talked to her mother. She felt a grin spread across her face. "We can still do it, Mom. I know how to make plum pudding! You can just sit in a chair and tell me what to do—it'll be fine."

"Of course it will," said Grandma Louise. "I'll be here to help too."

"Oh, I don't know. It can get very complicated," Amy's mother said.

"Nonsense," said Grandma Louise. "When Joe's dad was alive we made it every year. I could make it blindfolded!"

Amy's mother gave her father a thoughtful look. "I guess that could work. Joe, what do you think?"

"Well, that takes the cake," he laughed. "I guess you could call it a blessing in disguise! Amy? Mom? You really think you can do this?"

Amy and her grandma nodded enthusiastically.

"And Henry offered to bring the things we need?" he asked.

Amy's mother nodded. "He's going to pick up the recipe tonight. That's why he's coming over. He and Edith will be here at ten on Saturday with the ingredients."

Amy's father scratched his chin and surveyed his eager family. "This is crazy. I didn't think we could afford to make plum pudding this year. Now we're going to have a whole plum-pudding party!"

The twins leaped from the couch in unison. "Yay! Plum pudding, plum pudding—we're gonna have a plum-pudding party!" They danced around the living room.

Amy smiled and patted her mother's cast. Mom reached down and cupped Amy's chin with her good hand. "You're such a strong little girl," she said. "Now that I've got only one arm I'll really depend on you. Are you sure you're up to making plum pudding without me?"

"You'll be there helping me, right? So it'll be great." Amy smiled to herself. Her idea had worked better than she could have dreamed.

ON SATURDAY MORNING, AT TEN O'CLOCK SHARP, Abigail heard the doorbell ring. Mr. and Mrs. Winslow came into the kitchen, wearing matching Santa hats, escorted by the twins. Grinning like Cheshire cats, the Winslows carried overflowing bags of groceries into the warm kitchen and moved toward the table.

"Whoa!" said Henry Winslow when he saw Abigail. "Joe told me about your accident, but that's quite a cast!"

Abigail laughed and held up her broken arm. "Such bad timing," she said. "Luckily I have Amy and Louise to take my place. I'll be the drill sergeant. And we're sure glad you're both here to help. Boys, please hang up the Winslows' coats."

Henry and Edith unloaded all the bags onto the table and kitchen counters.

"Wow," said Amy, "looks like it's all there—even the suet!"

Joe brought the big plum-pudding bowls in from the garage and set them in the sink. "Henry, Edith," he said. "I can't tell you how much this means to us."

"And to us," said Edith. "Let's get started."

Abigail stood to one side and gave directions to everyone to bring order to the chaotic kitchen. She had Amy wash the bowls out while her mother-in-law and the twins unrolled cheesecloth and began cutting it in large squares about two feet across. "Put the squares in a pile over there," said Abigail, "so they'll be ready when we need them."

"Boys, when you're done with the cheesecloth, get your jackets on and come out back," said Joe. "You can help me shell the almonds on the picnic table."

"Before you do that, Joe," said Abigail, "run the bread and the suet through the hand grinder. You can attach the grinder to the picnic table so it won't make a mess in the kitchen."

"Okay," said Joe. "I've got the suet here—boys, bring the bread out when you come. Henry, why don't you join us out back? I could use your help."

Rob and Max grabbed their jackets off the kitchen hooks, then Louise gave them each two loaves of white bread. They clattered out the door. Before he followed the boys out to the backyard, Henry Winslow surveyed the kitchen and the women already at work. "Ladies, let me tell you again how happy Edith and I are to be part of this project. It's a plum-pudding *phenomenon*." He looked thoughtful. "I guess you know it gets kind of lonely for us at Christmas now that our son and his family are living in Florida." He smiled again and went outside.

Meanwhile, Amy divided three pounds of flour between the two bowls.

"Good, Amy. Now add the dried fruit to these bowls," Abigail said, before taking a sip of coffee. "Divide all the fruit into two parts, half in each bowl with the flour."

While Amy worked with the fruit, Louise half-filled two large canners with water and set each canner on the stove. She turned the burners on to medium.

Amy added all the dried fruit to the mixing bowls, sending puffy white clouds of flour above her head. "Oops!" she squealed, coughing and laughing.

"Silly girl," said Louise, wiping the flour off Amy's nose. She began scraping a large lemon over the grater and gathering the zest in a bowl.

"I love the smell of lemon zest," said Abigail, breathing deeply while the canners on the stove began to simmer, adding heat and humidity to the kitchen. "It always makes me think of Christmas."

Following Abigail's instructions, Edith dumped the brown sugar into the bowls containing the dried fruit and flour. Using a wooden spoon, she began stirring. Louise picked up another wooden spoon and stirred the other bowl until all the ingredients were mixed together. Amy then added lemon juice and zest, six beaten eggs, and two cups of milk to each bowl.

"Now you have your work cut out for you," said Abigail.

Louise and Edith began to stir once more. As the two older women worked, Amy slowly added the spices to each bowl. Soon the entire kitchen was filled with the aroma of a rich and heady brew of lemons, spices, and fruit.

Max opened the door for Rob, who walked slowly into the kitchen carrying a large bowl. "Here are the bread crumbs and nuts!" said Rob, handing the bowl to Amy.

"It smells like a candy store in here," said Max, as he handed his bowl to Louise. "But it's so steamy. Here's the suet. I'm going back outside. C'mon, Rob."

Louise divided the remaining ingredients between the two bowls while Edith and Amy stirred and stirred. When the ingredients in each bowl were completely incorporated, Amy called Max and Rob from outside and instructed them to wash their hands.

"Okay, you two," said Abigail, pointing to the stack of cheesecloth squares on the counter. "Take a chunk of this mixture and roll it into a volley ball-sized piece and place one on each piece of cheesecloth."

Edith Winslow pitched in to help the boys. When they were finished making the balls, Amy and Joe wrapped each pudding tightly in pouches of cheesecloth. Joe used butcher's string to tie the pouches to dowels which he hung over the simmering water in the canners. He used large sheets of aluminum foil as lids.

As he sealed up each canner he said, "Now, we just wait for several hours for the pudding to steam."

"So what do you think?" Abigail asked Henry and Edith as they began to help Amy clean up the kitchen. "Do you think you can do this yourself next year?"

"I think we have it," said Henry, "and if we have any problems, I know an expert I can call!" He winked at Amy, whose cheeks flushed as she smiled back at him.

THE NEXT DAY WAS A SPECIAL DAY FOR AMY because she was singing a solo with the junior choir for the church's annual Christmas program. But the excitement of the day was tempered by the fact that Amy still didn't know what to write for her school essay.

As he drove to church, Amy's father asked, "So when is this essay due, Amy?"

"Tomorrow. I still don't know what I'm going to write about."

"I know you," said Abigail, cradling her cast in her lap. "You'll think of something."

The junior choir had never sounded better. When it was time for her solo, Amy stepped in front of the other singers. The Colorado sunshine streamed through the stained-glass windows, bathing Amy in brilliant red, blue, and yellow beams as she began the timeless words of her solo:

What child is this, who, laid to rest, on Mary's lap, is sleeping?

Whom angels greet with anthems sweet, while shep-herds watch are keeping?

Suddenly, Amy forgot about her essay and the fact that her family traditions were not as exciting as those of her classmates. Caught up in the haunting melody of the song, she closed her eyes and offered up her solo as a gift to the baby Jesus, the Son of God who had been born in a lowly manger.

THAT AFTERNOON, HOWEVER, AMY'S WORRIES descended once again. Time was swiftly running out. What *would* she write about?

"Amy!" Her mother's voice came from the kitchen. "Please come in here for a few minutes. I need your help."

Mom was sitting at the kitchen table, surrounded by wrapping paper and gift tags. "Could you write out some plum pudding tags for me?"

"I guess." Amy sighed. "I can't start on my essay anyway until I decide what to write about."

"You'll figure it out," said Mom. "And this won't take long."

She gave Amy a list of names, starting with the Winslows, of course, and including the city mission, the firemen at Lakeview Fire House, residents at Meadowlark Nursing Home, children at the hospital, and Dr. Kellogg, among others.

As Amy wrote names on the tags in her neatest penmanship, she marveled at how many people would enjoy her family's plum pudding. She smiled to herself as she recalled the events that had taken place in the kitchen the day before. Making plum pudding had been so much fun. Even with her broken arm, Mom had laughed and been happy. The weight of sadness that Amy had seen on her father lifted as he worked with Mr. Winslow and the boys to make the pudding. The kitchen had smelled so sweet and spicy, and laughter had filled the room. Amy smiled. Plum pudding had put everyone in the Christmas spirit.

Suddenly, just like the sunlight that shone through the church windows that morning, the glow of an idea suddenly came over Amy as she finished the last tag.

"Mom!" she squealed in delight. "I just figured out what I'll write about! Now I gotta get started on my essay!"

"Told you you'd come up with something," her mother said, laughing. "Happy writing!"

It didn't take Amy long to finish her essay. She started by writing about her father's struggle to find a new job and her mother's broken arm. But then she wrote about plum pudding and the joy it brought to her and her family. She wrote about how the Winslows had helped them and they'd helped the Winslows and brought Christmas joy to others through their plum pudding. She wrote about the love her family had for one another and how making plum pudding wrapped all of that love together at Christmastime.

Our Christmas tradition, she finished, *is special because we give plum pudding to those we love and those whose lives need a little sweetness and spice. It makes everyone happy, and it's the way we show others how much we love them, not just at Christmastime but all year long.*

Amy read her essay out loud, then gave it a title as she recalled something Mr. Winslow had said when they were making the pudding.

AMY HANDED IN HER ESSAY FIRST THING MONDAY morning. "You seem very happy," Mrs. Anderson said as she took the assignment. "I hope you enjoyed the experience!"

The following weekend brought a rare and wonderful Colorado warm spell. Temperatures soared to a balmy seventy degrees, and Mr. and Mrs. Winslow invited the Norris family to come to their house for a pre-Christmas picnic. As they sat in the sunshine at the Winslows' large picnic table, the sky was blue and clear, and there wasn't a bit of wind. Mr. and Mrs. Winslow—wearing their Santa hats again—reached into a large cooler and unloaded baked beans, potato salad, cole slaw, and sandwiches of all kinds along with plenty of paper plates and napkins.

After the food was served, Mr. Winslow turned to Amy's father. "Would you say grace, Joe?"

Amy's father nodded. "Thank you, Lord, for this beautiful day and these wonderful people who helped us with our Christmas project. Bless this delicious food, our plum pudding tradition, and those gathered here together. Amen."

"Amen," said Amy along with the others. She began scooping potato salad onto her plate. "Well, I finally turned my essay in last week at school."

Amy's mother jumped in to explain. "Henry, Edith, Amy's talking about an essay she wrote for school about family Christmas traditions and why they're special."

"Right," said Amy. "And guess what I called it. 'The Plum Pudding Phenomenon,' just like you said, Mr. Winslow!"

"We're so proud of her," Amy's father added, then winked. "And not just because she won the essay contest." He tousled Amy's blonde hair.

Amy grinned and blushed. "Merry Christmas, everyone!"

"Merry Christmas!" they repeated.

And then everyone dug in to dessert—warm plum pudding with hot lemon sauce.

English Plum Pudding
(adapted from an old English baker's recipe)

3 pounds flour

1 pound bread crumbs

½ pound almonds, cut fine

2 pounds moist brown sugar

2 pounds suet

2 pounds seeded raisins

2 pounds sultana raisins

1 pound candied peel (lemon, orange, citron)

1 quart milk

6 eggs

2 ounces mixed spices—cinnamon, allspice, nutmeg, ginger, cloves

Grated peel of 1 lemon and juice of ½ lemon

Mix all ingredients. If mixture appears a little dry, add more milk. Form into four volley ball-sized balls and tie up in greased and floured cheesecloth and steam six to eight hours. (The smaller the puddings, the shorter the steaming time.)

Age the plum pudding in a cool place for at least a week. Peel the cheesecloth off and cut the pudding into chunks—it should be the consistency of a soft cheese. Serve as is, or warm slightly and serve with lemon sauce. If kept tightly wrapped in cool place, plum pudding can last up to a year. Serves forty to fifty, depending on serving size.

Finding Something Precious

Pam Hanson & Barbara Andrews

St. Joseph, Michigan, December 1932

Martha Warner looked down at the Christmas trees she'd drawn on a newspaper with her daughter's red and green crayons. Nine-year-old Caroline had long ago peeled off the papers and worn the waxy colors down to stubs, but they were all her mother had to work with. There was no money for the festive wrapping paper the dime store sold.

It was three days before Christmas, and times were hard. The Great Depression was in its third year, and families all across the country were struggling. Martha knew the paper dolls and small metal truck she'd managed to purchase weren't what her daughter and four-year-old Bobby really wanted for Christmas, but it had been a stretch to buy even those small gifts.

"Mom, I can't sleep," Caroline called from the apartment's only bedroom. "Bobby keeps poking me with his knees."

Martha hurried to shush her daughter before she woke her brother. Caroline needed a room of her own, but there was no alternative to sharing with Bobby. At least the children had a bed. Her own was a lumpy old davenport—one of the few pieces of furniture they'd been able to keep when their landlady, Mrs. Pratt, evicted them. Caroline was standing on the far side of the bed, looking frail in one of Martha's old flannel nightgowns, cut down to fit her.

"I want to go back home," Caroline said, crossing her arms and not bothering to whisper.

"Honey, please. You know we can't. The apartment and the restaurant were together. When we couldn't pay the rent on the restaurant, we lost the apartment too."

"I want Daddy to come home."

Caroline's voice sounded small and on the verge of tears, which would surely wake her brother.

"I miss him too, honey. And he's going to be back here with us soon."

"When? Why can't he come home for Christmas?" Caroline walked over to her mother and wrapped her arms tightly around her waist.

Martha felt her daughter's tears through her threadbare housedress but was at a loss to comfort her.

"We've talked about the Depression before," she said. "It's not always going to be like this. Someday, things will be better, and our family will be together again."

"Why can't we live on Uncle Stan's farm?" Caroline asked.

It was a good question, one Martha wished had a different answer. There was a vacant house—little more than a shack—on Uncle Stan's property, since Stan could no longer afford to pay the workers who once stayed there. But after Bill's parents sold the farm to Stan for next to nothing, without ever asking Bill if he might want a share, Bill had become doggedly determined never to seek their assistance, regardless of how badly his young family might need it.

"Uncle Stan has your cousins and Aunt Bonnie to take care of. He can't afford to support our family too," Martha said. "Now go back to bed. Tomorrow is the last school day before Christmas vacation. And I bet Miss Madison will have a little surprise for everyone."

It pained Martha she hadn't been able to send the ten cents Miss Madison had asked of each parent, though she had sent a few pennies she'd found in the couch. She knew the teachers were only being paid in script, pieces of paper they could redeem for food or other necessities, so even a kind, generous person like Caroline's teacher couldn't afford to pay for a party out of her own pocket.

"If Daddy can't come here, maybe we could go where he is." Caroline's voice rose, and Bobby stirred on the bed.

Martha put a finger to her lips. "*Shh.* Please—don't wake your brother." She took Caroline's hand and led her out of the bedroom, easing the door shut behind her. "I've told you before. We can't. Daddy shares one tiny room in a boarding house. There's no room for all of us."

"I could sleep on the floor."

"No, it's best we stay here." She hugged her daughter one more time and shooed her off to bed. "Remember, it's only two days until Christmas Eve. They'll turn on the tree lights for the service at church. You always love that."

After she tucked in Caroline for the second— and hopefully last—time that evening, Martha sank down on the couch, too exhausted to change into her nightgown.

"Oh, Bill," she said quietly, "I miss you so much."

The truth was, Martha couldn't share her real reasons for not joining her husband in Chicago. She'd only been there once, but in her memory it was a dark and frightening place. Shortly after Martha's parents died, her aunt Ada had taken her on a trip to Chicago in a motorcar as a special treat on her tenth birthday. They'd had lunch in the elegant tearoom at Marshall Field's Department Store, but the city had been a scary place, so crowded and noisy and confusing. And so dirty she'd had to scrub the soot from her face when she got home. Martha had felt lost and afraid, even in her aunt's care.

But crime had been the main reason Martha feared Chicago. Even though Prohibition had ended the year before, she had vivid memories of the gang wars and violent murders she read about in the usually staid St. Joseph, Michigan, newspaper. Now Bill was working as a scab, crossing often-violent picket lines daily in order to work in the plant.

Not wanting her children to fear for their father's safety, Martha never mentioned her real reasons for the entire family not going together to Chicago. It wasn't a place she would risk taking her children, no matter how much they missed their father. She hoped Bill understood, though he had often asked her to bring the children and join him there. But his job was temporary, until the strike was settled. Unless he found something permanent, it made sense for her and the children to remain in St. Joseph.

Martha slid off her davenport bed and got down on her knees, her hands pressed together in prayer.

"Dear God," she prayed, "please help us find a way for our family to be together again."

In Chicago, Bill Warner stood outside the soot-stained meatpacking plant, saying a prayer, as he did every morning, for the strength to get through another day at work. He loathed the stink of the factory and the blood that would soak the white duster provided by the company. But most of all, he loathed being away from his family. Even though Martha was good about writing whenever she could afford a stamp to mail a letter, the letters only made him miss his family more. He knew Bobby was growing like a weed, and Caroline was becoming a young lady right before her mother's eyes—and he was missing it all.

"Go home!"

"Scab!"

The picketers' angry voices yanked him from his thoughts.

"You're taking an honest man's work!" another shouted as he advanced toward Bill in a menacing way.

Bill hurried inside. He hated passing through the gauntlet of the picket line to get to his job, although so far the threats hadn't escalated past verbal. Truth was, he sympathized with the strikers, especially on the safety issues that made working in a meatpacking plant as dangerous as a battlefield. The company's owners had used these desperate times to take shortcuts at the plant and cheat workers out of pay every chance they could.

In the locker room, lit by a single dangling bulb, Bill took off his faded plaid jacket and hung it in his assigned slot, then set his lunch with it. His landlady packed him a nickel meal in a sack every day, but Bill had come to dread the contents. Her specialty was brown bread spread with lard, and it was often his only meal of the day. Hungry though he was, he only managed to choke down whatever she sent by remembering his family wouldn't go hungry or homeless as long as he had work.

"Morning, Bill." Fred Ferris hung his threadbare coat in his locker. "Heard anything about them reaching a settlement?"

It was the question the scab workers asked every day. If management settled with the union, their jobs would be lost. Like Bill, Fred had come from a town

many miles from Chicago when his factory job ended
not long after the stock market crash.

"Not yet," Bill said. "Hear anything from home?"

"My brother wrote to say they're not hiring anyone
else at the plant."

"That your older brother?" Bill asked.

"Younger. Sixty-two. He's going west to look for
work. Easy for him to go so far. He never married."

Bill knew his coworker had seven kids, two still at
home, and a daughter who'd recently moved back in
with her own three children after her husband walked
out. Bill knew the added burden of four more mouths
to feed weighed heavily on the older man. Sometimes,
thinking about Fred's troubles made his own burdens
seem light by comparison. But even so, he still missed
Martha and the children so much it hurt.

As Bill took his place on the line to begin process-
ing hogs, he thought about his brother, Stan, and the
family fruit farm. Bill wondered how different their
life would be if he'd fought for a share before his folks
sold it to Stan for a fraction of its value.

Hurt not to have even been offered a chance to buy
part of the farm, Bill had distanced himself from his
family, especially Stan. There had been no big fight,
yet relations were strained, with Bill stubbornly determined to make it on his own without their support.

Martha's night on the lumpy couch had been fitful and restless, and she woke with Bobby staring down at her in the cold morning light.

"What's up, big guy?" She pulled herself into a sitting position.

"My tummy hurts, Mommy." He crawled beside her and laid his head on her arm.

"Maybe you're just hungry," Martha suggested, knowing Bobby hadn't eaten much of yesterday's supper of boiled macaroni with bits of diced bologna.

She touched his cheek. His dark-brown hair stuck to his damp forehead. Her little boy was burning up.

"Oh dear," she said, the words escaping from her mouth before she cautioned herself not to alarm her son.

She tried to comfort him, first tucking him onto the couch with a cup of warm milk flavored with a dash of cocoa and sugar, then putting a damp cloth on his forehead and fanning him with a folded newspaper.

As Caroline got ready for school, Martha drew a tepid bath for Bobby and had him soak as the water cooled, hoping it would lower his fever. He whined and complained, but it was a weak-sounding whimper. By the time Caroline left for school, Martha knew her son's illness could not be ignored. She'd have to take him to see Dr. Jordon, even though that meant using the last of her money. She'd been saving to buy a chicken and a bit of butter for mashed potatoes for a special holiday dinner. Now even a nice Christmas dinner was out of the question.

She bundled herself and Bobby up and headed for the doctor's office. He wanted her to carry him, something he'd considered himself too much of a big boy this past year to allow. They reached the doctor's small office over the dry goods store on Main Street. It was crowded with coughing, sniffling people. In desperate times like these, no one went to the doctor unless their illness was too debilitating to relieve with home remedies or aspirin from the corner drugstore. In fact, she'd heard the pharmacist say few went to the doctor without checking with him first to see if there might be something else they could try. Anything to save a few cents.

Bobby hung limply on her lap, his hot forehead pressed against her. He was too sick to fidget. Normally, he'd have been bouncing around the room, but he drifted in and out of sleep as they waited his turn to see Dr. Jordon.

She watched, feeling helpless, as Doc felt Bobby's head, then under his neck, then listened to his heart and chest. Then he nodded and smiled.

"I've been seeing a lot of this," the older man said. "It seems bad, but it only lasts about twenty-four hours.

Forty-eight, tops. Give him plenty of liquids and half of one of these every four hours."

He handed her a paper packet filled with pink pills. They were nothing but aspirin with a couple added ingredients, but Martha had heard people insist they cured their ills. If they made Bobby feel better, she was grateful to get them. A trip to the drugstore was beyond her budget. She thanked the doctor and left with her sick child.

The walk home was only six blocks, but Bobby whimpered and lagged behind until she finally gave in and carried him, even though the snow stung her face and made the pavement icy and treacherous. By the time they got home, her back was aching. She was weary to the bone, the kind of tired sleep couldn't fix. She missed Bill more with each passing day, especially when the children needed his loving support.

That feeling intensified when Caroline came home from school in tears.

"Dick and Ted took my cookie!" she sobbed. "We got it for the Christmas party, and I was saving it to share with Bobby."

This wasn't the first time those mean brothers had picked on her daughter. Martha wished she could go and talk to their mother, but she couldn't leave her children home alone to do it. Even if she had a telephone, she had no family nearby she could call to stay with them.

Weariness draped over Martha like a heavy blanket, weighing her down. She felt hopeless. She couldn't go on this way.

She looked from Bobby to Caroline. He was ruddy-faced and glassy-eyed, yet appeared more alert than he had earlier. He was on his way back. Caroline, however, looked completely distraught and at the edge of tears.

"I have an idea!" Martha said. "How about we make cookies?"

Caroline sniffled. "I thought we didn't have any sugar."

Martha walked to their tiny kitchen and looked in the jar. There was maybe a tablespoon of sugar. She looked in the flour bin. A few cups. She had a smidgen of baking soda. A single egg. Pat of butter.

She hated to deplete their larder on something as frivolous as cookies, but her children needed a happy distraction and so did she. As they mixed the few ingredients into a bowl, each taking their turn with the whisk and improvising as they went since there was no recipe for ingredients as sparse as theirs, the chatter intensified.

Bobby was dusted with flour, but his eyes shone with something that wasn't fever-related as he hand-patted his bit of dough as flat as he could.

Caroline chattered as she hadn't done for a while, and for just a moment life felt wonderfully normal. Then Martha noticed a tear leaking down her daughter's face. Before she could ask what was wrong, she heard a small sob escape Bobby's mouth.

"I miss Daddy," Caroline said.

"Me too," said Bobby.

"Let's make him a cookie," Martha suggested, desperate to keep her children from being so sad.

"But, Mommy, we can't give it to him. He's too far away. I don't think he's ever coming back." Caroline's lip quivered.

"Hush now!" Martha said. "He's coming back! I promise. This is just for a little while, until things start to get better."

Nothing she said could cheer her children. To make matters even worse, the cookies turned out tasteless. Even cold milk couldn't make the dry baked goods better since Martha needed to save the last of it for breakfast.

She tried to entice them into making paper snowflakes, but that only reminded them of the funny failed snowflakes Daddy had tried to make with them last Christmas. She read them a story, but it was one that Daddy read better. Nothing she attempted worked at getting their minds off what—or who—they were missing. Without their father, all was bleak.

When the children were finally asleep that night, Martha went to her dresser and pulled out a seed-pearl necklace—the "something old" her aunt Ada had given her when she and Bill married. It had belonged to Martha's mother, and to her mother's mother before her. It was the only thing Martha owned that her mother once wore, and even though it probably wasn't wildly valuable, it was likely worth more than anything else they owned.

Possibly even worth as much as three bus tickets to Chicago.

Though the idea of Chicago frightened her, Martha realized being without Bill had begun to scare her even more. She and the children needed him, even if it meant moving somewhere dirty and dangerous. She needed to trust that God would take care of them. She needed to have faith.

Martha put on the necklace for what she knew would be the very last time and looked at herself in the mirror.

"I'm sorry, Mama," she said, touching the tiny pearls with her fingers. "I hope you understand."

BILL SAT ON THE SIDE OF HIS COT, RUBBING HIS stiff neck. His roommate's snoring was horrifically loud, but Bill doubted that was to blame for his sleeplessness. It was more his thoughts that kept sleep at bay. Even though he'd dropped into bed thoroughly exhausted from his fourteen-hour day at the plant, he'd been unable to turn off his brain.

He'd been going over and over the loss of the restaurant, which had been doing well enough to keep them afloat until Mrs. Pratt, the building's owner, had increased the rent. It simply was more than he and Martha could afford to pay. Their confrontation had been brief and unpleasant. Bill had refused to beg to his landlady, though now wished he had, wondering if his pride might not end up destroying his family. He should have pleaded his family's case with Mrs. Pratt in a more effective way. On top of that, he'd been unwilling to go to his brother about possibly living, and helping work on, the farm. Instead, he'd come all the way to Chicago, leaving his wife and children behind.

Mrs. Pratt had been unyielding about the increase. Since he and his family lived in the apartment upstairs from the restaurant, he'd not only been suddenly out of work but homeless as well.

And now, here it was, Christmas. And he was away from his family for the first time ever.

There had to be more to life than merely existing. He labored away at the plant six days a week to send home so little money it barely kept their heads above water. What he made scraping by would never improve their situation.

Bill stared down at the only item of value he owned lying in his hand, a gold pocket watch that had belonged to his father. It had been a peace offering, given to him after his parents sold the farm to his brother for next to nothing. Bill hadn't wanted the watch, but his dad had insisted.

He'd promised his father he'd never sell it, and he'd kept that promise, even when money from that watch might've meant saving their business.

And now here he was, watch in hand, planning on breaking that promise.

"My family will always mean more than a thing," he said out loud.

It was crazy to walk away from a job in times like these, but he needed to have faith that the Lord would provide. He needed to believe his family needed him every bit as much, if not more, than ever. He knew what he had to do, and it started with swallowing his pride.

"I put my trust in You, Lord," Bill said quietly. He stood and dressed, then gathered all his meager belongings into a bag and took one last look around the room. He'd lived here for months, but it could never be home. Home was miles away, in a shabby little apartment. Not in a place, but with his family. So Bill started the long journey home.

MARTHA HAD EXPECTED THE CHILDREN TO BE upset about leaving town, about moving far from the only life they'd ever known, but they'd surprised her by happily helping her pack.

"Can I run and say good-bye to Miss Madison?" Caroline asked. Caroline's teacher lived in the boardinghouse just across the street.

Martha glanced at the time and nodded. "But hurry! We don't want to miss our bus."

"Can I go too?" Bobby asked.

"Only if you promise to hold Sissy's hand and do what she says," Martha said.

Once they were gone, Martha packed away the final few items and then began cleaning the tiny apartment. She was just beginning to get nervous about how long it was taking her children when they came bursting through the door.

Despite the damp cold, Caroline carried her coat like a bundle. And something was wrapped in it.

"Mommy!" Caroline cried. "You have to help her. She's hurt."

Martha took the bundle and laid it gently on the floor. Inside was a beautiful long-haired calico cat, its hair matted in places with mostly dried blood, front leg dangling and clearly broken.

"She must've been hit by a car," Bobby said.

"We found her against the curb, under a whole lot of old newspapers," said Caroline. "They'd blown up over her, and then I guess they got wet and sort of stuck. I don't think she could get out from under them, so no one knew she was there."

Martha filled a basin with warm water and began cleaning the cat. Except for her broken leg, the cat's wounds appeared fairly minor.

The cat lay still as she tended her, seeming to understand that Martha meant her no harm. She didn't even try to bite when she tugged at her front leg until the bones aligned.

"Can you find me a pencil to use as a splint?" she asked her children. "And some rags so I can tie it in place."

By the time the leg was secured, the cat had started purring. The kids brought her some water and a few tiny bits of hard cheese. She ate hungrily—purring the whole time.

"She must have felt so scared," Caroline said as she stroked the cat's head. "And I bet Mrs. Pratt has been worried sick about her."

"Mrs. Pratt?" Martha asked.

Caroline and Bobby both nodded.

"This is her cat," Bobby said. "I'm pretty sure it is, anyway."

"Don't you remember Precious, Mommy?" asked Caroline. "She was always in the window at her flower shop."

Martha looked again at the cat, picturing her clean and surrounded by blooms. It certainly looked like Precious, down to the black pirate patch around her left eye.

Mrs. Pratt adored that cat, called it her baby. Much as Martha disliked the spoiled and greedy Mrs. Pratt, and even though that awful woman was responsible for her family's situation, she still couldn't find it in herself to not return this animal that she knew meant the world to her.

"She must've accidentally gotten out of the shop," Martha said. She checked the time and then glanced around the apartment for something to put the cat in.

"If we hurry, we can drop her off on our way to the station," Martha said.

SELLING THE WATCH HAD BEEN EASIER, AND FAR less painful, than Bill had anticipated. It was a means to an end, and at that end was his family.

"Please, sir," said a woman at the front of the bus. "Could you just stay in your seat for a while? Your pacing is driving me to distraction. You won't get there any faster by walking."

"I've been gone a long time," Bill said, taking his seat again. "Guess I'm a little excited."

"Going home for Christmas?" asked the man seated across the aisle from Bill.

"Going home for good," said Bill. "Couldn't find work at home so I had to go to the city, but I'm finally headed back."

"Lucky you," said the man. "Finding work isn't easy, especially when you're living somewhere else."

"Actually, I don't have a job to come back to," Bill said. "But I couldn't stay away from my family any longer. I know it's crazy, in times like this, but I have faith the Lord will take care of us. That He knows how important it is for a family to be together."

If Bill had to put his pride aside and go to his brother and beg to stay in the old caretaker's one-room shack on the farm, that's what he would do. It was time to make peace anyway. He understood now, more than ever, the importance of family.

"I'm not sure if you're a brave man," said the man, "or a foolish one."

"I have faith," Bill said again. "God will provide."

Each time he said it, he felt the assurance growing inside him. He and his family would be fine. God would provide and show him the way.

WHEN MRS. PRATT SAW WHO WAS AT HER DOOR, she looked instantly annoyed. "What?" was all she said when she opened it.

Martha almost felt sorry for the unpleasant, pinched-looking older woman. Almost. This wasn't the upper-class neighborhood in which Mrs. Pratt had grown up and to which she was accustomed, but like most everyone in the country, she'd fallen on tough times. Just not as tough.

"I believe we found something of yours," Martha said.

Caroline lifted the corner of the box, and Precious meowed.

"Oh!" Mrs. Pratt exclaimed. "Precious!"

Martha had never seen tears pour so quickly or in such a gush.

"I thought I'd never see her again," she said. She looked from Martha to the children, then back to Martha again. "And of all the people to find her..."

"Would you rather we hadn't found her?" Martha asked. "Are we that distasteful?" Martha knew those were un-Christian words for her children to hear her say, but she couldn't help herself.

Mrs. Pratt shook her head no, but instead of explaining, she lifted Precious carefully from the box and held the cat to her chest.

"I raised her from the time she was this big," their former landlady said, holding her fingers just a few inches apart. "I found her on my stoop, no mother around. She was shivering, eyes barely open. I fed her milk from an eyedropper."

This woman might be a terrible person, Martha thought, but there had to be something good in her to have such love for a cat.

"She's been missing for over a week," she said. "I looked everywhere."

"We found her under a whole bunch of wet newspapers," Caroline piped up. "Her leg is broken and she's kind of banged up, so I guess she couldn't get out."

"She's pretty weak," Bobby said. "We never would've found her if my ball hadn't rolled to a stop exactly where she was, and then we heard her meow."

"It was kind of a miracle," Caroline said. "We could barely hear her."

Mrs. Pratt nodded, tears spilling each time her head dipped.

"Please. Come in," she said. "Get out of the cold."

"We only have a minute," Martha said. "We're on our way to the bus station."

"We're going to be with Daddy!" Caroline said, the excitement clear in her voice.

"Because we miss him so much that we cry all the time," Bobby said.

"*We* don't cry all the time," Caroline said. "Just you. And that's 'cause you're still a baby."

Bobby swatted at Caroline but missed. She stuck out her tongue.

Martha shot them a stern look, and they stopped.

"Sorry," Martha said. "They're excited. He's been gone since... well, you know how long."

Mrs. Pratt cast her eyes downward, likely uncomfortable from the reminder. While looking down, she spotted her purse, which she reached for.

"Here. Let me give you children a reward," she said. "Having Precious back means the world to me."

The children looked at each other, then at their mother. Martha shrugged. It was up to them.

"Thank you, Mrs. Pratt," Caroline said. "But we helped her because it was the right thing to do, and Daddy always told us we needed to look out for each other. Love thy neighbor."

"Don't forget 'do unto others as you'd have them do unto you,'" Bobby said. He sounded so grown-up that Martha felt tears form in her eyes.

There was an awkward silence as the children's words hung in the air. Mrs. Pratt looked down at the floor again.

"We need to get going," Martha said. "We've got a bus to catch, don't we, children?"

Bobby jumped up and down, clapping.

"Can I at least drive you to the station?" Mrs. Pratt asked hesitantly. "It's so cold and windy, and it's starting to snow."

"That's okay," Martha said. "It's really not a bad walk."

Mrs. Pratt reached out and took Martha's hand, and then squeezed it.

"Please," Mrs. Pratt said.

There was something in her voice that reached Martha's heart. "That would be nice. Thank you."

As they rode to the bus station, it crossed Martha's mind that she'd likely never see Mrs. Pratt again after today, a realization that enabled her to be bolder than she might otherwise have been.

"So if you don't mind me asking, how's our old restaurant doing?" Martha asked.

Mrs. Pratt let out a long sigh. "To be honest, not so good," she said. "Serves us right, I suppose. Pete's working it all by himself now. We can't afford to pay anyone, and working there—it made me feel dirty. And not the kind of dirty you can wash off, if you understand what I mean." She looked up briefly, met Martha's eyes for just a moment, and then looked down again. "I just manage the flower store now. Pete does the restaurant. Well, he *tries*."

Martha wasn't sure what to say. The Pratts had raised the rent on the restaurant so much there had been no way she and Bill could afford to keep it. But rather than close the restaurant, the Pratts simply kept the business going as if nothing had ever happened.

And put Bill, Martha, and their children out on the street.

"These are tough times. I'm sure it'll get better eventually," Martha said.

They rode in silence for the next few blocks. When Martha looked over at Mrs. Pratt, there were tears rolling down her cheeks.

"We don't deserve for anything to get better," Mrs. Pratt said. "Last Sunday, Pastor Boyd preached his sermon on the importance of repenting and making restitution for your wrongs, and Pastor's words—they were like hooks in me. I haven't been able to shake free of them. I keep thinking about what he said, and about what Pete and I did to your family. It was wrong, and I'm so sorry."

"I forgive you," Martha was quick to reply. Her words surprised herself. Did she really forgive Mrs. Pratt?

But Martha's heart felt lighter from those three simple words she'd spoken. Forgiving Mrs. Pratt was an antidote to the angry poison that had brewed inside Martha for months. Martha smiled, thinking how perfect a day it was to forgive, on this, the eve of Jesus' birth.

Yes, the Pratts had done wrong by them, and it had cost them greatly, but now their family would be together again. Somehow, some way, it was going to be fine.

Mrs. Pratt was crying again, and much harder now than before. She pulled the car into a parking spot by the crowded bus station. The snow was falling heavily.

"Thank you for the ride," Martha said. "We never would've made it here in time if you hadn't driven us."

"Thank you for saving my cat," she said. "I'm sure you wouldn't have been rushed if you hadn't taken the time to take care of her and bring her back to me."

"Merry Christmas!" Caroline told her as she and Bobby scooted from the back seat. Martha handed them each a bundle to carry.

The three of them hurried across the bustling station toward the ticket window. It seemed everyone in the state was traveling home to be with family for Christmas. Martha grew impatient at the long, slow-moving line at the ticket window. As she and the children waited, they heard a car's horn, blaring away.

Caroline turned and tugged at her mother's hand and pointed. Martha saw someone waving.

"It's Mrs. Pratt," Martha said. "We must have forgotten something in her car."

Martha glanced over their belongings and didn't see anything missing, but Mrs. Pratt was waving so urgently that they headed back. She sighed at the delay. She just wanted to get their tickets and get on the bus and on their way to Bill.

And then suddenly she saw her beloved husband and the father of her children sitting in the passenger seat of Mrs. Pratt's car. A confused look crossed his face as he got out of the car.

"Daddy!" The children yelled in unison and raced the rest of the way to him, leaping into his arms. Martha dropped her bags and ran too.

He held them all, bundled tight in his arms.

Mrs. Pratt spoke first. "I saw him walking by just seconds after you left," she said. She laughed. "I grabbed him by the arm and yelled at him to get into the car and sit down and then started honking my horn."

"I thought she'd lost her mind," Bill said.

"How easily we could've missed you," Martha said. "We were headed to Chicago."

"I quit my job there," Bill said.

"I gave up our apartment here," said Martha.

"Sold my watch to get here," Bill said.

"Sold my pearls to go there," said Martha.

It wasn't at all funny, but they both started to laugh.

"You have a place to stay here," Mrs. Pratt said. "And maybe a business to run, or help run, if you'd like."

Martha and Mrs. Pratt filled Bill in on what had happened, and the situation with the restaurant. And how none of it would've been possible if Caroline and Bobby hadn't first found Mrs. Pratt's injured cat.

"I feel the Lord gave me a chance to make this right," Mrs. Pratt said. "This happened for a reason. We didn't land in each other's paths today without cause."

Bill told them about the leap of faith he'd taken, how he'd trusted in God to provide. And God had.

"Well, now He's providing your family with a place to stay," Mrs. Pratt said, "and my family with a chance to right our wrong."

"Does this mean we get to all be together as a family, Mommy?" Caroline asked.

"It certainly does," Bill said, answering for her as he scooped Bobby up onto his shoulders and hugged Caroline. Martha thought her heart would burst with happiness and joy as she stood closer to her husband.

"Merry Christmas, Mrs. Pratt," she said, taking the older woman's arm and bringing her into their tight-knit circle.

"Let's get out of this cold and back to your home," the older woman said.

They piled into Mrs. Pratt's car and rode away from the station and toward their new old life. Times were tough and would continue to be, Martha knew, but as long as they had each other, and the grace of God, there was hope.

THE LETTER

Debbie Lynne Costello

Savannah, Georgia, December 1945

Benjamin Davis pulled his gaze from the letter in his hands and gave his attention to his wife, Sharon. Maybe there could finally be some reconciliation between his wife and daughter-in-law.

Sharon huffed. "She must want something. We haven't heard a word from her since Richard went off to fight in this wretched war."

Benjamin's hopes wavered. "That's not true, dear. She contacted us when Richard went missing."

His wife tipped her chin, a habit she had whenever talking about their daughter-in-law. "I would hardly consider a one-line missive, *Your son is missing and presumed dead*, to be contacting us. She was most likely required by some military law to inform us."

His gaze drifted back to the letter in his hands. Sharon might not be happy about Jennifer and the children's planned visit, but he was ecstatic. It had been far too long since the laughter of young voices filled these rooms. He'd feared he'd never hear them again with his son dead and Jennifer and Sharon unable to remain in the same room without a drastic temperature drop.

"I think I'll call her."

"Yes, why don't you? See if all she wants is money." Sharon patted her coiffure. "We can send that without her coming."

He made his way to the telephone stand and picked up the phone. His gut lurched as he dialed. The last time he'd called this number, his son had been on a news assignment, covering a plane crash of two airmen on St. Simons Island. The next phone call was Richard saying he was headed off to war. He drew in a deep breath as his thoughts went back in time. He'd been thankful when he'd received a letter from Richard saying he'd been stationed with Jake Powers, an old buddy from high school, and they'd look out for each other.

The receiver rang in his ear, bringing him back to the present. He glanced at his wife as the ringing continued. After four more rings, he placed the handset back on the cradle. "No answer."

"What is that woman doing out at five o'clock? She should be home fixing dinner for her children." Sharon sank onto the sofa. "Honestly, does she have no maternal instincts in her?"

Benjamin grinned. "You mean like all the cooking you did for our boys?"

Sharon raised her brows. "I supervised and made sure there were healthy meals on the table."

"I know you did, dear. I'm just teasing."

The corners of her mouth quivered, then turned up. "I could have done it myself if not for heading up so many of the community charities." She sighed. "And had Richard not gone off and gotten himself involved with *that* woman, I could be working alongside my daughter-in-law on worthwhile needs right now."

"Andrea is a fine young lady, but Richard didn't love her. Besides, Jennifer is lovely if you'd give her a chance."

"Jennifer will never be...oh, never mind. We'll just have to agree to disagree, dear. Richard could have done so much better for himself. But for your sake and the memory of our son, I'll put aside our differences if she must come."

BENJAMIN PULLED BACK THE CURTAIN IN THE front room window for the umpteenth time, waiting for Simon, their handyman and driver, to pull up in the car with his guests. He missed his son. Jennifer and the grandchildren were his last family.

He let out a huff of air as the sheer fabric fell from his fingertips, covering the window once again. He'd had such high hopes when Jennifer's letter had arrived, asking if she and the children could come spend the week of Christmas with them. The poor girl sounded exhausted when he'd finally been able to get in touch with her. She was so tired she seemed confused about who sent whom the letter.

JENNIFER NEVER DREAMED SHE'D BE MAKING this trip to her in-laws' house without Richard.

She pushed her fingers through seven-year-old Cassie's fine blonde hair as her daughter slept, blissfully ignorant of what the week might bring for her and her younger brother. Richie slept with his head against the locked car door, his tawny mop looking as if she'd not made him comb it in over a week.

She stared out the window, ignoring the view of old oak trees covered in Spanish moss whizzing by. Pinpricks stung the back of her eyes as memories of Richard's parting words flooded her mind. *"I'll be back before you even know I'm gone. And if you need anything while I'm gone, Dad and Mom will be there for you.*" If she hadn't been so frightened watching her husband go off to war, she'd have argued with him that his parents would never reach out to her. And they had proved her right...until now.

A chill crept up her spine. Her father-in-law had waited three years to reach out to her and his grandchildren. So why now? What if they hoped to take her children from her now that Richard was gone?

She reached into her pocketbook, careful not to disturb Cassie, and pulled out a worn, lace-trimmed handkerchief. Dabbing her tears, she reminded herself that she was doing this for Richard. He'd always wanted her and his parents to reconcile, and since Benjamin had extended the first olive branch, she would accept it for her husband. After all, it was only a week. Surely the three of them could survive that.

It was times like this she wished she'd learned how to drive. She had never needed to when Richard was alive, and after he left for the war, she told herself she'd learn as soon as he got back and could teach her. But now that he wasn't coming back, she'd have to ask someone else to teach her. She never wanted to be in a situation again where she had to rely on the Davises to get where she needed to go. It didn't matter that they'd invited her. She'd have much rather driven Richard's old car, which had been sitting in the driveway for the past three years.

The driver turned down the tree-lined road leading to her in-laws' house and pulled to a stop in front of the antebellum brick home with a double stairway leading to a columned entrance portico.

Cassie woke and rubbed her eyes. "Mama, are we at the president's house?"

Jennifer blew out a puff of air. "No sweetie, just someone who thinks she's the first lady."

"THEY ARE HERE!" BENJAMIN YELLED OVER his shoulder as he hustled out the door to meet his daughter-in-law.

Simon had opened Jennifer's door by the time Benjamin reached the car. She stepped out and turned to help the children out as well. With her arms wrapped around Cassie and Richie, Jennifer faced him looking like a mama dog protecting her pups.

"Jennifer, it's so good to see you." Benjamin opened his arms, encompassing all three of them.

"You too, Benjamin." Jennifer stepped back from his embrace.

Benjamin squatted down and gave Cassie a hug. Her wavering smile tugged at his heart. He straightened and turned to Richie, roughing up his hair. His heart twisted. Richie looked so much like his Richard had at that age. The sparkling blue eyes full of mischief, the slender nose, and the ears that looked too big for his head.

"I bet you all are starved after that ride," Benjamin said.

The children nodded in agreement. Jennifer shifted her stance. "I don't feel much like eating."

"Let's go see what the cook can put together for you two young'uns...that is, if it's okay with your mom." Benjamin turned to Jennifer.

"Thanks for asking, Benjamin. I'm sure the kids would love a snack."

"I don't want to do anything to upset you. If I step on your toes, don't be afraid to say something."

"I know, Ben. *You've* always been kind to me."

Benjamin cringed inwardly. He'd always loved Jennifer, but he'd allowed the tension between her and his wife to cloud his judgment and to put up a wall between them. He should have attempted reconciliation between the two women years ago when Richard was still alive.

"Mama, why would Grandpa step on your toes?" Richie gazed up at his mom with innocent eyes.

"It's a figure of speech, honey."

Benjamin looked at his daughter-in-law. "He remembers I'm his grandfather?"

She smiled. "I told them when you came out of the house."

He nodded and stuck out his hand, waiting for Richie to clasp it. "Let's go see if we can find some food."

They headed up the sidewalk. Sharon met them in the large open foyer, her back straight and her chin tipped. Benjamin bit back a sigh.

"Jennifer, it's good to see you and the children." Sharon's words sounded forced. She crossed her arms.

Jennifer gave a curt nod. "I appreciate your opening your home to us."

At this rate it wasn't going to be easy getting the two women to soften up to each other. It truly would be a Christmas miracle for them to see past their differences.

"Richie, Cassie, this is your grandmother." Jennifer wrapped her arms around the children even though Benjamin still held Richie's hand.

"Hello," the kids said in unison.

"It's nice to see you again, Cassandra and Richard." Sharon gave them a small smile.

Richie looked up at his mother. "Are we in trouble?"

"No. Why would you ask that?" Jennifer's brows furrowed.

Richie pulled his hand from Benjamin's and cupped his mouth. Standing on his toes, he stole a quick glance at his grandmother and whispered, "She called me Richard."

Jennifer bit her bottom lip. "That's your proper name. You're not in trouble."

Sharon mumbled that there was a reason they were called proper names.

Benjamin decided he might as well throw the two women together and let them start working out their differences. "Why don't you two ladies relax in the parlor, and I'll have tea sent in to you. Or do you prefer coffee, Jennifer?"

"Tea is fine."

"I'll have Simon put your bags in Richard's old room. That way the children can have the rooms on either side."

"They may want to sleep with me." She drew the children closer to her.

Sharon let out a quiet but unladylike snort.

Benjamin smiled, hoping to ease Jennifer's fears. "Whatever you want is fine. I'm going to get these two little imps something to eat."

JENNIFER FOLLOWED SHARON INTO THE PARLOR, glad her mother-in-law wasn't walking behind her, judging her every step. She took the seat closest to the door while Sharon found a seat more to her liking. With her heart thudding loud enough to drown out any voice, Jennifer took a deep breath as she stared across the room at the woman looking down her nose at her.

The silence lengthened even as squeals of delight floated down the hall. Jennifer's gaze followed her nose to the fresh-cut pine branches adorned with red and silver bulbs that decorated the mantel. She scanned the rest of the room. A porcelain nativity set, intricately painted, graced a round table in the corner of the room. Garland scalloped the top of the walls near the ceiling, and an angel with open arms stood over a baby Jesus on an end table.

"I don't believe I've ever been here when the house was decorated for Christmas."

"You haven't. We've never had the privilege of seeing our only grandchildren at Christmastime." The society matron nailed Jennifer with her gaze.

And whose fault was that? Richard had always avoided coming due to the way his mother treated his wife. "The Christmas season is always busy for journalists. They cover all the extra social events on top of their regular schedule. It was hard for Richard to get away, let alone travel over an hour to get here."

"He should have gone to school to be a doctor like he'd planned."

"And you think doctors don't have to work over the holidays? People get sick regardless of Christmas." She shouldn't have said that. She'd made this trip to mend the rift that had developed, not to add to it.

A slender, middle-aged woman wearing a light-gray cotton gown trimmed with white cuffs and collar entered the room with a tray.

"I'll take that, Mrs. Hilton." Sharon pushed herself up from the chair and retrieved the tea tray.

The woman gave a nod. "Thank you, ma'am." She exited the same way she came in.

Sharon poured a cup of tea. "Sugar and cream?"

"Please. Two lumps."

Her mother-in-law plopped the two sugars into the tea along with the cream and stirred.

Jennifer reached out for the offered cup, realizing too late Sharon would see the oil stains. She took the tea, sending the saucer and cup into a shaky dance of rattling, thus drawing scrutinizing eyes.

"What is that all over your hands?" Sharon's brows knitted together.

"Oil." Jennifer took a sip of the steaming tea.

"Oil!" Sharon sounded horrified. "Don't tell me you change the oil in your car."

"No. I don't drive." Jennifer took another sip of her tea, hoping against hope that would be the end of it.

"How, pray tell, did you manage to get your nails and hands covered in that black—"

"I had to go to work. Richard's military pay wasn't enough to cover the bills and keep a family."

"What kind of work could you possibly do that makes your hands look like a man's?" Sharon raised her palm. "No. Don't tell me."

She'd taken a job at Savannah Machine and Foundry, building and converting ships for the US Navy. It made her feel closer to Richard, knowing she was doing something for the war effort. Even so, she was certain her mother-in-law wouldn't approve.

BENJAMIN STOOD IN FRONT OF THE BEDROOM mirror and tightened the double Windsor knot of his tie. "You've had two days with Jennifer, and I don't believe things are getting any better between you two."

Sharon twisted a fallen strand of hair and stuck a hairpin into it. "You would think she'd put a little more effort into being nicer, since she is the one who initiated this visit. It makes me wonder if I was right in the first place and she's only here for money."

"Let's be fair, dear. You haven't actually been Miss Hospitality. You treat her like a second-class citizen."

"She's…different than we are. Richard never should have married her. They were poles apart. Did you see her hands when she arrived here? Heavens!

How does a woman stand to have nails caked in black grease?" She gave a fake shudder.

"First, Richard and Jennifer may have come from different social standings, but they got along fine—even when outside pressures worked against them. Second, have you talked to Jennifer about her work?" He raised a single brow.

"Why should I? It obviously isn't anything I'd approve of."

"I give the young woman a lot of credit. She went to work, knowing full well she could have come to us and asked for money. But she didn't come begging. She did what she felt she had to do."

"And have you noticed the children's behavior because of it? They act like wild animals. Why, last night they came tearing through the dining room screaming like banshees and nearly knocked over my Tiffany vase." She turned her back to him. "Will you zip me up, please?"

He tugged on the zipper and chuckled. "You'll have to blame me for that, dear. I was having a little fun with them. I told them the first one to find where I'd left my pocketknife would get a quarter."

"You shouldn't encourage bad behavior. I'd bet those kids haven't had a day of discipline since Richard left. I hate to think what kind of grades they get in school. I imagine they come home from school and do whatever they want because their mother is at work. What kind of life is that for children?"

"You're jumping to a lot of conclusions. They seem like perfectly normal kids to me. I could get used to having them around."

"*Hmm*. That might not be a bad idea. If Jennifer can't care for our grandchildren and give them the opportunities we can..."

"Sharon, I don't want to hear another word. Our daughter-in-law is doing a fine job raising those kids. You won't be adding any more stress to that young lady's life. Do you hear me?"

She opened the bedroom door. "Whatever you say, Benjamin."

JENNIFER HESITATED AS SHE WALKED PAST THE only door in the house that had remained closed since she arrived. She glanced behind her and, for the second day in row, tried to turn the knob. It didn't budge. Why on earth did they keep the door locked? Did Sharon put her valuables in there for fear she or the children would steal them? It was obvious Sharon saw her as lower class and apparently untrustworthy too.

Jennifer drew in a deep breath. This visit was for Richard. His parents were all the kids had left of their father. She didn't even own a picture of Sharon and Benjamin.

Steeling herself for what the day would bring, Jennifer headed downstairs to the dining room.

Sharon looked up from her seat at the table. "Good to see you awake early."

"Good morning." Jennifer went directly to the buffet and put some scrambled eggs on her plate.

"I've been meaning to tell you that we're attending a Christmas party tomorrow evening. You'll need to be ready promptly at seven o'clock."

Avoiding her mother-in-law's intense stare, Jennifer took her seat at the table, wishing Benjamin was there. "You and Benjamin go on without me. I didn't bring anything to wear." She didn't own anything that would be acceptable for Sharon's circles.

"Nonsense. I know a young lady who looks about your size. I'm sure she'll be happy to lend you a gown."

Jennifer squirmed in her seat. "Thank you, but the children are too young to leave alone. You go and have a good time."

"I won't hear another word. Mrs. Hilton will stay with Cassandra and Richard."

"They go by Cassie and Richie."

Sharon ignored her. "I'll tell Mrs. Hilton to plan on staying late to take care of the children."

GETTING READY FOR THE PARTY, BENJAMIN cocked his head and glanced at his wife, who bore the same curious expression that he felt. Piano music? "The Liberty Bell" by John Philip Sousa was floating through the house.

He followed the melody with Sharon at his heels. They entered the formal living room, and Sharon sashayed ahead of him, every bit as beautiful as the day they'd married. Ready for the Christmas party, she wore a shimmering silver gown that showed off her trim figure.

She stopped next to the black lacquered grand piano, staring at her granddaughter as the child's hands glided over the keyboard. Benjamin came up to stand beside Sharon as Cassie's fingers stilled.

Big blue eyes stared up at Sharon in wonder. "Mama said you thought you were the first lady, but I think you look more beautiful than any first lady, Grandmother."

Sharon flinched. Benjamin held back a chuckle. Out of the mouths of babes. He turned to glimpse the hem of a green gown pass by the archway and head down the hall.

Sharon smiled. "Thank you, Cassandra. I wasn't aware you could play the piano. Who taught you to play so beautifully?"

"Mama."

"Your mother?" Her voice cracked. She turned to Benjamin. "I never would have guessed."

"She teaches us French too," Cassie said proudly.

"You don't say?" Benjamin grinned. "I wonder what other secrets your mother is hiding from us. Speaking of your mother, do you want to come tell her good-bye before we leave?"

Jennifer was kneeling down, hugging Richie, when they reached the front door. Cassie gave her mother a hug. "Oh, Mama! You look more beautiful than any first lady too."

Jennifer gave a sheepish grin. "Thank you, sweetheart. You two be good for Mrs. Hilton, you understand? I don't want to hear that either of you have gotten into mischief."

The young mother did look stunning. Benjamin found himself wishing Richard could have seen his wife looking so breathtaking. Every single man would have his eyes on her tonight.

"Really, Jennifer, they are only children. Don't expect too much out of them." Sharon ran her hand over Richie's unruly hair.

Benjamin raised a brow at his wife. She shrugged. Jennifer continued to speak with the children as he helped Sharon with her coat.

He leaned in, putting his lips to his wife's ear. "Having a change of heart?"

They got to the party early enough to park just two houses down the street. Benjamin went around and opened the ladies' doors for them. One beautiful woman on each arm, he headed toward the Bingleys' Christmas party, sure he'd be the envy of half the men.

BY EIGHT O'CLOCK THE PARTY WAS IN FULL SWING. A charity auction for war victims was to follow dinner.

Jennifer was surprised at how much she was enjoying herself. The people she'd met were friendly and made her immediately feel comfortable. Sharon had actually stayed by her side and included her in conversations with her friends. And Benjamin stood only a few feet away, visiting with the men. Her heart flipped. Maybe there was a chance for their family after all.

A beautiful young woman with brunette hair piled high on her head strolled up to Sharon.

"Andrea," Sharon said, "I'd like you to meet Jennifer, my daughter-in-law. Jennifer, this is Andrea. Her family and ours go way back."

"Nice to meet you." Jennifer smiled.

The woman seemed to be sizing her up and Jennifer suddenly wondered if she was as pretty as Cassie had claimed.

Andrea leaned toward Sharon. "When you asked for my dress for the Christmas party, I thought it was for the auction, not a charity case."

Jennifer didn't bother to look if Sharon had a smirk on her face. She spun on her heel and headed for the nearest exit.

No wonder Sharon had acted so nice to her. She wanted to humiliate Jennifer in front of all her friends—let everyone know that she wasn't good enough for Richard. Andrea may have acted like the comment was meant just for Sharon, but she'd said it loud enough for anyone standing nearby to hear.

Tears bit at the back of Jennifer's eyes. She'd wanted to do the right thing. She'd wanted her children to have a part of their father through their grandparents, but it was too hard. Maybe when they got older they could visit without her. But right now all she wanted was to go home.

She pushed out the door, not bothering to get her coat. She could walk the ten or so blocks back to the Davises' house...if she could remember her way.

She hustled down the steps and turned onto the sidewalk. She hadn't made it past Benjamin's car when his voice rang out in the cool air.

She wrapped her arms around herself and turned. Benjamin took off his jacket as he rushed toward her.

He wrapped it over her shoulders and opened the car door. "Ready to go home?"

She nodded, afraid her voice would betray her.

He climbed in the car and turned it toward his home. "I'm sorry."

"Don't be. You tried. I knew when I received the letter wanting me to come that you were the one behind it. Sharon will never accept me. She blames me for Richard's choice of career. All I did was support my husband in what he wanted to do with his life, and I'd do it all over again. The truth is, I'll never be good enough for her son, even in death."

Benjamin opened his mouth as if to say something and then stopped. Jennifer turned to gaze out the side window. She would pack when they arrived. In the morning, she was leaving.

He pulled up to the curb in front of his house. Even the beauty of the old home told her she could never be a part of this family.

Benjamin came around and opened the door. "I'll get your coat when I pick up Sharon."

"Thank you." She started toward one of the curved stairways.

"Jennifer, if it makes any difference, I heard Sharon defending you when I left. She wanted to come, but I told her I thought it would be better if I came back to get her."

Jennifer hurried up to the door, not sure what to believe, but knowing she'd overstayed her welcome.

The house was quiet—the children probably already in bed. She tiptoed up the stairs.

At the top she turned to go to her room, but the locked door sat slightly ajar. Her heart sank. The last thing she needed was for Cassie or Richie to have broken in while she was gone.

She planned to pull the door shut, but instead she pushed it open just enough to peek inside. The room was dark. She flipped the switch and gasped as she pushed the door completely open and walked inside.

It was like a shrine—to Richard.

She walked along the walls and ran her hands over the frames. There had to be hundreds of articles—articles written by Richard. This wasn't the room of a mother ashamed of her son.

Jennifer turned to fully encompass the room. A drum table in the corner held her and Richard's wedding picture. She picked up the frame and hugged it to her chest.

"Oh, Richard. I can't do this without you."

BENJAMIN FULLY EXPECTED TO SEE BAGS PACKED and waiting by the door when he returned from the party. Sharon couldn't have been sorrier about how things had turned out.

His gut knotted. To think his wife had finally seen the gem that Jennifer was—only too late. He doubted Jennifer could ever forgive Sharon or believe the fiasco was not intentional.

He put his hand at the small of Sharon's back as they headed up the stairs to their bedroom. Muffled sobs came from within Richard's room. Sharon hesitated, turning to Benjamin with tormented eyes. She raised her fist. He nodded. She tapped on the door.

He heard a sniff. "Who is it?" Jennifer's voice warbled.

"It's Sharon and Benjamin. May we come in?"

Silence.

"Please. We want to make this right."

Another sob broke loose. Benjamin opened the door and crossed the room. Jennifer sat in the corner in a chair, her knees pulled up to her chest, still in her borrowed gown. He opened his arms and she flew into them.

"*Shh,*" he whispered into her hair. "We are here for you."

Sharon moved next to Jennifer and patted her back. "I'm so sorry, Jennifer." Sharon choked. "I've been terrible to you. I was just so sure I could do a better job picking out a wife for Richard, but I was wrong. He did a fine job, and I couldn't be prouder. Tonight, Benjamin shared with me how proud he was of you for going to work when Richard went off to war. You could have come to us and asked for money, but you wanted to do it yourself. And then when I heard Cassan—Cassie playing the piano tonight, I realized how hard you must have worked to keep food on the table, keeping up with all the responsibilities of a household, and still made sure our grandchildren were accomplished in some of the finer things in life. I had to ask myself, could I have been the woman you have grown to be? I am ashamed to say I don't think I could have withstood the pressures you have had these past years. Please forgive me."

Glistening tears streamed down his wife's face. He'd never been so proud of her.

"Oh, Sharon." Jennifer let go of Benjamin and swiveled to hug Sharon. "All these years I've resented you for not supporting Richard's choice of career, but tonight I...I noticed your locked room's door ajar, and I went in. And I saw you've kept every article my husband wrote. You've been more loyal to him than I have. I never even thought to keep any of his articles."

Benjamin wiped the tears from his eyes and wrapped his arms around the two most wonderful women he'd ever met.

The following morning was glorious. Jennifer and Sharon chatted at the breakfast table as he played a game of I Spy with Cassie and Richie, a fairly new game the children had never heard of and thoroughly enjoyed.

Through the day Sharon kept sneaking off by herself, and Benjamin worried her happiness wasn't sincere. Thankfully, Jennifer didn't seem to notice anything amiss. Instead she'd asked him to take her to town to finish her Christmas shopping.

BENJAMIN CHUCKLED AT THE CHILDREN'S delight as they ripped through their last wrapped gift, then sped off, playing with their new toys. It was a wonderful Christmas.

Jennifer retrieved two still-wrapped presents from under the tree, handing one to Sharon and one to him. "They're from me. It isn't much, but I wanted to do something."

Benjamin opened his package to reveal a pocketknife.

"I know it isn't as nice as the one you had, but the children told me you'd lost yours."

A lump rose in his throat. "It's perfect. I'll be sure not to lose this one." He gave her a hug.

"Your turn, Sharon." Jennifer smiled.

Sharon opened her gift. "I love chocolate! I've hardly had any since the war."

"Richard mentioned to me how much you liked it."

"Thank you. I'll savor each bite." Sharon placed a present on Jennifer's lap. "From me."

Jennifer tore through the paper to find a large book and flipped open the cover. Her hand flew to her mouth and tears filled her eyes. She turned the pages. "These are Richard's articles."

"I put them in a scrapbook—something I thought would be more manageable for you."

Jennifer enveloped her mother-in-law in a hug just as the doorbell rang.

"Who on earth could that be on Christmas day?" Benjamin strode to the door.

Two young men stood on the porch, both in uniforms. Despite one's gaunt, pale face staring back at him, Benjamin's legs nearly collapsed beneath him.

"Richard?" *How could this be?* "Glory to God... Sharon! Jennifer, come quickly!" He threw his arms around his son.

Shouts and tears of joy filled the house as Jennifer and Sharon rushed forward. Smiling, Richard assured them he was not only alive but well, despite some obvious changes in his appearance. He introduced his friend Jake amid frenzied hugs and tearful greetings. Finally, they all sat down, Richard balancing both of his children on his lap.

Benjamin sat on the edge of the couch. "We were told you were missing and presumed dead. What happened?"

"I was wounded"—Richard glanced at his arm stump—"and picked up by the enemy. It took a while for news of the war's end to make it to where I was being held. When I was finally released, I couldn't go home." He looked at Jennifer. "Not like this. How could I support you and the children?"

Tears glistened in Jennifer's eyes. "We love you. We'll manage."

"I didn't know what to do, so I went to see Jake. He's the one who talked me into coming here today."

"Son, we'll help in any way we can."

"You can still be a journalist. It's what you're good at," his mother urged him.

Richard hung his head, and the brightness of the moment dimmed. "I can't type, Mom."

Sharon patted Jennifer's arm. "I bet your talented wife could do it for you."

Richard blinked. "Did you just call Jennifer talented?"

"I've learned a lot about your wife this past week. I see why you chose her over my own pick. She's a wonderful daughter-in-law."

Richard scratched his head, wonder, as well as hope, rising in his green eyes.

Jake grinned. "You got my letters, then?"

"Letters?" Richard frowned.

"As our pact required, when I thought you had died, I sent letters to your wife and your parents to set up a reconciliation," Jake told his friend. "I wasn't sure it would work, but I had to try, since that was your dying wish. That's why I brought you here, in the hope Jennifer had come."

"So, Jake, you were behind the letters." The pieces fell into place for Benjamin.

"Letters? You knew there was more than one letter?" Jennifer asked.

Benjamin nodded. "Like my son, I wanted nothing more than to see our wives reconciled. I wasn't about to do anything to upset that boat. So I kept the fact that you clearly thought I had sent you a letter when we had received a letter from you to myself."

"You're a wise man, Dad."

Benjamin turned to Jake and shook his hand firmly. "You've not only brought me back my son, you've given me a daughter-in-law and two grandchildren! Not one, but the two best Christmas gifts I could ask for."

A FATHER'S GIFT
Keli Gwyn

Meadow Lake, California, December 1866

A sharp cry from above sent the chisel in Cole Foster's hands crashing to the floor. *Molly!*

He sprinted through the workshop, dodging the bureau he was building, and took the back stairs two at a time. It couldn't be happening again. Could it?

Heart thundering, he reached the bedroom. One look at Molly's ashen face gave him his answer. They were going to lose another baby.

His sweet wife's wobbly smile told him she knew it too.

"I'm sorry, Cole. I didn't mean to startle you." She swayed and slung an arm around a column on their four-poster bed.

He willed himself to remain calm. If she sensed his concern, she'd worry about him. Right now she had to think about herself and their baby. He rested his hands on her shoulders. "What happened?"

Hope shone in her warm brown eyes. Despite having endured three miscarriages, she wasn't one to give fear a foothold. Her inner strength far exceeded his. Surely God would grant someone as good and faithful as Molly the desire of her heart. She'd make a wonderful mother.

"I had a twinge and thought it might have been a labor pain. I'm sure I'm wrong, but as a precaution, I should probably take to bed for the duration. Unfortunately, dear husband of mine"—she drew as near as her rounded belly would allow, rested her palms on his chest, and peered at him through fluttering lashes—"that means you'll have to take over my chores."

He'd do anything for her. He kept his tone light. "Are you sure you're up for my cooking? You remember the last time I tried my hand in the kitchen." How could she forget? He'd ruined a perfectly good pot roast.

She laughed, a light, airy sound without a hint of censure. "You did your best. I'll just make sure not to invite any of our friends to share a meal while you're doing the cooking."

"You'll get no argument from me." He regretted the words immediately. Molly had the gift of hospitality and had never met a stranger.

Her playfulness fled. She sank onto their bed and smoothed her skirts. "I don't know why you insist on keeping your distance from our neighbors. You weren't like this before."

"Things were different. The people back home cared about one another. They weren't consumed with dreams of striking it rich."

Hoards of people had flocked to the Meadow Lark area intent on one thing—finding gold and making their fortunes. They didn't care who was hurt when they left their homes and families behind.

Molly was quick to defend the townspeople. "A few are like that, perhaps, but everyone I've met is nice. Look at how they've been helping one another tunnel between the buildings."

He sat beside her, the feather tick sinking under his weight. Her long brown braid brushed his shoulder. "They have no choice. With all the snow we've had, that's the only way to get around."

The ground floor of his uncle's furniture store and workshop was buried beneath a blanket of white. Cole had to light a lantern whenever he worked downstairs. At least the upstairs windows weren't covered yet.

Being confined to Meadow Lake and to this building day after day was driving him mad.

His ever-patient wife hadn't uttered a word of complaint. "I like it. The bright white light streaming through the windows is so cheery."

"It is. On the rare clear days between storms, anyhow."

If only he'd been able to head down the mountain to the fertile Central Valley, far from the mining claims. He was eager to settle on the parcel of land his uncle was helping him buy and start his own farm. But with Molly due to deliver soon, he had no choice but to stay put.

Before Uncle Ralph had headed for his winter home down in Sacramento City, he'd delivered a large load of lumber, filled the woodshed, and ensured that the pantry held plenty of food—provided one liked beans and biscuits. Thankfully they had several dozen jars of Molly's delicious preserves.

She swatted his arm playfully. "Come now. We have much to look forward to. Our little one will be here soon. Maybe even by Christmas, if my calculations are correct."

More likely their baby would arrive far too soon, if Molly had already begun having labor pains. Babies born a month early didn't fare well.

Molly would be on his mind and in his prayers morning, noon, and night until their little one arrived safely.

LYING ABED, WHILE NECESSARY TO KEEP THE labor pains at bay, had grown tiresome. Molly shifted her position, sank back into the puffy pillows, and concentrated on her guest, one of the few other women in town. The talkative miner's wife, Bernice, rocked her sleepy baby girl while recounting tales of her husband's valiant search for the gold believed to be embedded in as-yet-undiscovered quartz veins.

While Molly understood the drive of the fortune seekers, she felt for those, like this mother, who spent countless hours alone. Mining wasn't an easy life. It put a strain on a family. In Cole's case, his father's desire to get rich had led him to leave his wife and sons in 1849 and head for the gold fields, where he'd met his death a year later.

Molly thanked the Lord that Cole loved the land and what he could grow on it rather than the treasure others hoped to find buried within it. Farming suited them both.

Once this harsh winter was over and they had their own place down in California's fertile Central Valley, they'd be content. For now, they must make the best of the present situation and trust their future to the Lord.

Molly corralled her wandering thoughts and returned her attention to Bernice. The freckle-faced woman had changed subjects.

"Ambrose is going to teach me to swim when it warms up. He says since we're living by a lake, I ought to learn, so I'll be out in it splashing around. Won't that be a sight?"

"I'm sure your lessons will be interesting." Molly admired the adventurous young woman. She seemed willing to accept the challenges of life in a harsh environment.

Bernice shifted her yawning daughter to her shoulder and rubbed the little girl's back. "I'm looking forward to them 'cause that means this infernal winter will be behind us. I never seen one as bad as this. Ain't you getting tired of it?"

"I'd welcome a taste of summer, yes."

"Wouldn't we all?" Cole entered, bearing steaming-hot cocoa and golden-brown biscuits with an assortment of spreads. His cooking had come a long way in a week. He set the tray on the bedside table and left.

"Your fellow sure keeps to himself, don't he?" Bernice asked.

"He's been busy helping me." While that was true, so was Bernice's observation. It wasn't like Cole to withdraw, but that's what he'd done ever since they'd arrived in Meadow Lake. He was cordial while waiting on his uncle's customers, but the warm, generous man she knew and loved had gone into hibernation.

She wanted to believe he was simply anxious about the baby. She certainly was. Once their little one arrived, perhaps Cole would relax, put the past behind him, and be willing to extend the hand of friendship. She prayed that would be the case.

"SURE. I'LL SWAP A CHICKEN AND A DOZEN EGGS for some of your wife's preserves. That'll make my sweet tooth happy." The burly mine owner shook Cole's hand, sealing their deal. "I'll drop them by on Christmas Eve."

Cole's plans to surprise Molly on Christmas Day were coming together. With the chicken from Mr. Stone, a jar of pickles from the livery owner, and potatoes and onions from Bernice, Cole would have what he needed to make a luncheon on par with any Fourth of July picnic—save one thing. Even though he'd put the word out, none of the few residents wintering in town had responded. He wouldn't be able to serve the lemonade Molly loved.

Mr. Stone examined a china cabinet in a far corner of the shop, opening every door and drawer and getting on his knees to peer at the underside. His inspection complete, he stood and brushed off the sawdust clinging to his trousers. "You make this, son?"

"I did."

"Thought you were a farmer, not a carpenter."

Cole was used to questions about his qualifications. "Farming's my vocation, but woodworking is my hobby."

"Hobby, you say? Well, this is some of the finest workmanship I've ever seen. The missus is going to join me next year, and I promised her I'd have a nice place. I've got the house, but it's a mite bare inside. How'd you like to spend your winter building the furniture to fill it, young man?"

An entire houseful of furniture? And not just any house. Mr. Stone had one of the largest in town. Cole had expected to spend the time they were snowbound without making a single sale, so this was welcome news.

The proceeds from this order would enable him to pay off the loan for his land more quickly than he'd hoped. "I don't know what to say, sir. I'm speechless."

"Say you'll do it."

Cole smiled. "Yes. By all means. Shall we discuss what you have in mind?"

The moment the door banged shut behind Mr. Stone, Cole bolted up the stairs and burst into the bedroom.

Molly gazed at him, wide-eyed. "Land sakes, Cole. What's the matter?"

"Nothing bad." He recounted his conversation with Mr. Stone. In his excited state, the words tumbled out.

She shot him a knowing smile, her bright blue eyes twinkling. "Isn't it wonderful the way the Lord provides? Here we are in the midst of a mining town buried beneath several feet of snow, and yet He's blessed you with the order of a lifetime from one of our new neighbors. Maybe now you'll agree that they're nice people."

Leave it to his persistent wife to use this windfall to teach him a lesson. "An order of this size is always appreciated."

"Even from a mine owner who entices men away from their families in order to search for gold?"

Cole strode over to their bed, leaned against one of the posts, and folded his arms. "I know what you're up to, Molly Foster. You expect me to forget about what happened and move on, but it's not that easy. You had a wonderful family with two parents. My ma worked far into the night washing and ironing other people's clothes just to put food on our table. If Pa hadn't left, things would have been much better."

"Would they? The way I hear it, your father was going to make his fortune, build a fine home, and send for all of you. But he walked past a saloon one dark night and took a bullet intended for someone else—before he'd had time to make good on his promises."

He sank onto the edge of the bed beside her. "I've never heard that. How do you know?"

She averted her gaze and toyed with the lace on her white nightgown.

Lifting her chin with a fingertip, he forced her to look at him. "Did Ma say something to you before she...passed?"

"Your uncle told me."

"Uncle Ralph told *you* and not me? Why?"

"There's no need to get sore about it." She rested a hand on the fist he hadn't realized he'd formed. He stretched his fingers and twined them with hers. "He knows how you feel about your father and thought I'd be the best person to tell you."

Uncle Ralph meant well, but how could he have kept that information from his own nephew? "What else did he say?"

She sighed. "That he hopes you can put the past behind you and find some peace."

He narrowed his eyes. "There's more to the story, isn't there?"

"My dear Cole." She slipped her hand from his and caressed his cheek. "I love you, but you can be a bit stubborn at times."

She did know something, but he knew her well enough to know she wasn't going to tell him. "I know a man has responsibilities, and he shouldn't shirk them. His wife and children depend on him."

"They do, but sometimes he has choices to make. Suppose I needed help. You'd go for it, wouldn't you?"

"Of course." A thought struck him with the force of a steel stamp crushing ore. "You're not telling me it's time, are you?"

She shook her head, smiled, and patted the mound at her middle. "Our little one seems content to stay put for now." She grew serious. "It's time to move on. If you'd stop keeping the people here at arm's length, you'd see how good and well intentioned they are."

He would if he could, but he couldn't bear hearing about others like Mr. Stone who had left their families behind. How could a man walk away from his own kin—even for a season?

A COMMOTION OUTSIDE WOKE MOLLY FROM HER afternoon nap. She sat up and scooted over until she could see out the south-facing window. A crowd had gathered around a tall man with a face as black as soot. He stood on two long, narrow boards and held an equally long pole in his hands. Planting it in the snow, he pulled a large bag from his back, opened it, and reached inside.

"Cole!" she hollered loudly enough for him to hear her over the rasp of his handsaw. He'd been down in his workshop all day, busy working on Mr. Stone's order.

He was up the stairs in no time. "Are you all right?"

She watched the activity outdoors. "I'm fine, but I'd like to know what's going on and who that man is."

"I'll find out." He donned his overcoat, lifted the window sash, and stepped out the second-story window onto the snow nearly level with it, sinking up to his knees with every step he took in the fresh powder.

Molly eagerly awaited his return. Having someone come into town during a winter like this was quite an event. Surely the visitor would have news. While her world revolved around waiting for their baby's birth, it would be nice to hear what was going on elsewhere.

Several minutes went by with the tall stranger passing out what appeared to be mail to the people clustered around him. Those who received something rejoiced, their shouts carrying through the crisp, chilly air.

She shook off a twinge of sadness. There would be nothing in that mailbag for Cole or her. Between them, they had only one remaining relative, and his uncle Ralph wasn't one to put pen to paper.

But they had each other and, the good Lord willing, would soon add another to their little family. She'd be content with what they had rather than pining for more.

The tall, thin man in the mackinaw jacket strapped the bag onto his back, doffed his hat to those assembled, and swooshed on the narrow boards across the glittering snow in the direction from which he'd come, the long pole gripped in his hands for balance.

Cole headed to the house, accompanied by Bernice, who cradled her baby girl to her chest. He lifted the window sash, stepped into the room, and helped the beaming young mother inside. They brushed off the snow and slipped out of their wet coats and boots.

"I've brought you company," Cole said.

"What a nice surprise. It appears you're having a good day, Bernice."

"I sure am. I got a letter from my aunt back East." She waved an envelope in her free hand. "Would you mind holding little Eva so I can read it?"

"Not at all." Molly opened her arms. Bernice placed the darling girl in them, sat in the rocking chair off in the corner, and savored the news from her relative.

Cole planted himself on the bed beside Molly and watched intently as she removed the blankets bundling Eva. Knowing him, he was worrying about their little one instead of trusting that all would be well.

"So who was that gentleman?" she asked him.

He jiggled the baby's hands, bringing forth peals of laughter. "They call him Snowshoe Thompson. He's been carrying the mail from down in Placerville over to Genoa, Nevada, for the past ten winters. Since we're having such a rough one, they've asked him to come our way this year too."

"Why does he blacken his face like that?"

"I reckon it's to keep it from burning due to the glare from the snow." He stared out the window at the spot where the unexpected visitor had been and smiled. "Those snowshoes of his—or skis, as he calls them—are really something. Each one is made from a single piece of oak. They're a good ten feet long and are tapered from their four-inch wide upturned tips to their slightly narrower backs. He straps them to his feet and has attached wooden blocks to support his heels."

Leave it to Cole to notice every detail of something made of wood. "That's quite the journey he makes. It's a long way from Placerville to Genoa."

"Ninety miles, I'd say, but he makes the trip east in three days. Amazing, isn't it?"

The rocking chair scraped on the wooden floor as Bernice dragged it over next to the bed. "What amazes me is that even though Snowshoe Thompson took a wife this past spring, he leaves her at home in order to make these trips so we can get mail. Folks 'round here say he's one of the most generous, selfless people you'd ever want to meet. Those who can, pay him a dollar for bringing their letters, but I heard tell he ain't been paid a cent by the postal service so far. He's a real hero, if you ask me."

"He certainly sounds like one." Molly's curiosity got the best of her. "Did you enjoy your letter?"

Bernice grinned. "Sure did. My aunt tells me my baby sister's married now and that she and her husband will be coming to California in the New Year."

Cole gave a firm nod. "That's the way it should be. A family should stick together, no matter what. You ladies would probably like to chat without a man around, so I'll get back to work."

"Thanks for coming upstairs when I called," Molly said.

"Anything for you, my lovely wife." He brushed a kiss across her forehead and left.

Bernice took Eva from Molly and rocked the little girl. "Your feller sure is taken with you, ain't he? But what was the other about?"

Molly chose her words carefully. "He appreciates the special bond a family has."

"I see. Someone who meant a whole lot to him left. That's it, ain't it? I understand. My pa came West back in 1849, but he had the good sense to see that the gold didn't come easy. He only stayed long enough to earn his passage back. Don't know what I'da done if he hadn't come home."

Bernice's perceptiveness surprised Molly. "I'm glad your father returned. I imagine it would have been difficult for those whose fathers didn't." There. She hadn't betrayed her husband's confidence, even though her friend's supposition was correct.

"Well, at least Mr. Foster has you. Perhaps if he was to give the rest of us a chance, he'd see that we ain't bad folks."

That was Molly's wish as well.

MR. STONE SHOOK HIS HEAD IN DISBELIEF. "You saw those snowshoes of Thompson's one time and made a pair just like them, huh? Is there anything you can't build, Mr. Foster?"

Cole shrugged off the compliment. "I needed a way to get your furniture from my shop to your house. I thought using skis as runners for a delivery sled would work."

"That they do." The brawny mine owner pulled on a pair of leather work gloves. "You're only two weeks into the job, and yet you've already got two pieces of furniture built. I'm impressed. Let me help you get this one inside."

The next hour passed in a flurry of activity as they got the parts of the bed frame into the master bedroom and returned to the furniture shop. They wrangled the wardrobe up the stairs, out a second-story window, and down the road to Stone's place.

Just as they set the large clothes cupboard down, a shout rang out.

"Snowshoe has made it again!"

Mr. Stone rubbed his back. "That's one sturdy piece of furniture. Glad we got it in when we did. A body can't miss a visit from John Thompson."

"You go on, sir. I'll see to my sled. It's not like he'll have anything for me anyway."

"Nonsense. We'll return the sled later. Right now it's time to witness the spectacle. Come on."

Not wanting to appear rude, Cole followed Mr. Stone to the south end of town. As was the case two weeks before, a crowd had gathered around Snowshoe Thompson.

The recipients of the handful of letters Thompson passed out rejoiced. He reached in the mailbag one last time, produced a paper sack, and called out a name.

Cole's name.

Cole blinked. "Me? There must be some mistake. He doesn't have anything for me."

Mr. Stone chuckled, his breath forming white puffs in the chilly air. "Seems you're wrong about that, son."

Curiosity sent Cole over the packed snow toward the mail carrier.

Thompson held out the lumpy parcel. "Here you go, Mr. Foster."

"Thank you, sir."

He opened the bag and gaped. It was full of lemons, at least a dozen of the bright yellow beauties.

Cole looked into the piercing blue eyes of the fair-haired Norwegian. "I don't understand. I didn't order these."

Mr. Thompson smiled. "I heard you wanted some."

"I did. I mean, I do, but—" He reached into his pocket and pulled out a handful of coins. "What do I owe you?"

"Nothing. One of your neighbors took care of it."

"I see." He didn't, but he'd learned all he could from the kindly mail carrier. "Thanks again."

Cole checked to see if anyone was watching the interaction, but the townspeople were headed back to their homes.

Perhaps Mr. Stone had arranged this. After all, he was happy about his new furniture. No, it couldn't be him. He'd placed his order after Thompson's previous visit and wouldn't have had a way to get word to him.

If not Stone, then who? Cole looked from person to person. It could be any one of them, really, since he'd put out word around town.

It would take some doing to solve the mystery, but he wouldn't rest until he knew who was behind the unexpected kindness.

NOTHING SMELLED AS GOOD AS A FRESHLY CUT evergreen. Molly handed Cole the last of the ornaments she'd inherited from her mother. Seeing them brought back wonderful memories of Christmases past.

"Could you fill that gap on the upper right?" she asked, pointing.

Her handsome husband hung the tiny drum on an empty branch, stepped back, and surveyed the bedecked tree. "It looks good."

"Indeed it does. I can't believe you spent so much time digging in the snow to find a small tree, but I appreciate it. I couldn't bear the thought of having you chop the top off a larger one."

"Anything for you, sweetheart. Are you ready to see the baby's bed?"

"Oh yes. And then I'll show you the clothes I've made."

Instead of giving gifts to one another, they'd agreed to use their time and talents creating items for their little one. Seeing the bed he'd built for the first time would make this Christmas special.

Cole went downstairs and returned carrying the most beautiful cradle Molly had ever seen.

"Oh, Cole! You've outdone yourself." The head- and footboards were scalloped, and he'd carved embellishments into both. "You must have spent a great deal of time on this."

He smiled. "Only the best will do for our baby."

"But how did you get it done? You've been busy with Mr. Stone's order."

"I, um…" He swallowed, his Adam's apple bobbing. "I built this last summer."

"Really?" Her skin tingled. "You believed everything would work out this time, didn't you?"

He nodded.

"So did I. Even when the pains began and I had to take to bed, I never stopped hoping. And now our dream's coming true. We're going to be parents." She blinked to clear her blurred vision.

"Oh, Molly. My dear, sweet Molly." He sat and pulled her into his arms.

A pain gripped her, and she squeaked.

He drew back, his face drawn. "What is it?"

"I think I felt a contraction, but I'm not sure. This one wasn't like the others."

He raked a hand through his dark, wavy hair. "Are you saying the baby's coming? Now?"

"Well, not just now, but soon. I think rather than having me show you the clothes, you'd best go for Bernice."

"Of course." He threw open the window sash, hopped out, and took off running—as well as he could, knee-deep in snow.

The window flew open again moments later, and he scrambled inside. "I forgot my overcoat, and it's freezing out there." He gave a shaky laugh. "I guess I'm not thinking straight."

She smiled. It did her heart good to see his excitement. After all this time, he'd finally be a father.

The next five hours were some of the longest Molly had ever endured. The contractions grew closer and more intense until she thought she couldn't bear another. Between each agonizing wave of pain, she listened for the voices below, where Ambrose and baby Eva waited with Cole. Her dear husband must be beside himself with worry. Lord willing, it would all be over soon.

The mantel clock in the parlor chimed twelve times. Christmas Day.

Time seemed to stand still, but Molly heard a single chime mark the half hour. She could barely catch her breath between the contractions. Another one seized her. Despite her desire to remain strong, she cried out.

Bernice offered encouragement. "It won't be long, Molly. The next time a pain comes, bear down as hard as you can."

She did, gripping the sheets and pushing with all her might.

And then everything changed. Their baby was here!

She fell back against the pillow, panting.

"You did it! You have a baby boy. I'm going to give him a swat to get him breathing on his own."

The smack was followed by a lusty cry, the most wonderful sound Molly had ever heard.

"I need you to take this little feller while I finish up."

She held her son, so intent on him that everything else faded.

Footfalls sounded on the stairs, rousing her. The door creaked open, and Cole peeked in. "I heard a baby cry. Is everything all right?"

Molly smiled. "Yes. It's all over. Come see your son."

"It's a boy?" The awe in Cole's eyes mirrored the sense of wonder that had come over her when Bernice placed the squirming boy in her arms.

"He's beautiful, isn't he?"

"Handsome, Molly. He's handsome." Cole held their son's tiny hand in his. "And small."

"What are you going to name him?" Bernice asked.

Molly focused on the boy in her arms and braced herself for Cole's reaction. "I'd like to call him Robert, and Bobby for short."

He recoiled. "No! Absolutely not. My son will not bear my father's name."

She persisted. "What if I told you that your father owned the property that's to be ours and had planned to move all of you out West as soon as he could?"

"What are you saying? Uncle Ralph owns the land."

"He owns half of it, yes, but the other half is yours now."

Cole shook his head. "You're not making any sense. You know as well as I do that Uncle Ralph bought the property for me and is expecting repayment of the loan."

"That's what you believed, and he chose not to correct you. He was afraid if he'd told you the truth, you wouldn't have come out West."

Bernice hovered over them. "I don't mean to interrupt, but if you'll hand me the little feller, I'll clean 'im up for ya."

Molly reluctantly relinquished her son and faced Cole. He'd folded his arms and was staring into the distance. "If you'll open my top bureau drawer, you'll find the deed underneath everything."

He sat with his eyes closed and his mouth moving as he carried on an unspoken conversation. Was he praying or fuming at his father?

His eyes flew open. He glanced at their baby boy in Bernice's capable hands, crossed the room, and yanked open the drawer with such force he nearly spilled its contents. Rummaging through Molly's unmentionables, he found the document and tilted it toward the lantern.

She waited for some sign, but Cole stared at the paper for the longest time, giving no indication of his thoughts. Surely he wouldn't refuse his inheritance. A prime piece of California's farmland would ensure them a good life.

"Here's your son, all freshened up." Bernice placed the precious boy in Molly's arms, now clothed in one of the outfits she'd made. "Ambrose and I will take Eva and head on home, but if you need anything, come get me."

Cole spun around. "Thank you, Bernice, for everything. I have a special Christmas dinner planned, and I thought you and your family might like to join us."

Bernice eyed him warily. "Are you sure you want us here for that? I thought—"

"Yes, I do." He cast a glance at Molly. "*We* do."

She rejoiced inwardly. Cole had taken the first step toward accepting the townspeople. "He's right. We'd love to have you join us. Please, say you will."

Bernice darted her gaze between them. Seemingly satisfied, she gave a curt nod. "Well then, we'd be delighted to share your meal." They agreed on a time, and she left.

The parlor clock chimed twice before Cole and Molly placed their son in his cradle, climbed into bed, and prepared to get some sleep themselves.

Cole gave her hand a squeeze. "Merry Christmas, Molly."

"Merry Christmas, Cole."

She waited, but he said nothing more. Their baby boy, still unnamed, lay in his bed beside theirs, his breathing even. Soon his father's soft snoring drowned it out.

What would the morning bring? Would Cole let go of his anger and accept his father's generosity, or would he hold on to the bitterness that had been eating away at him ever since he was young?

A WHIMPER WOKE COLE. IT TOOK A MOMENT for the unusual sound to register. He had a son—a healthy, hungry son, it would seem. That made sense. From the angle of the sun, it had to be well past eight.

Carefully, so as not to wake Molly, Cole slipped from beneath the covers. He padded around the bed to the cradle where the wide-eyed boy flailed his fists and scrunched his face. He was sure to wake his mama if he let loose with the wail that seemed imminent.

"It's all right," he whispered. "Papa's got you." He picked up his son and nestled the little fellow in the crook of his arm. "There's not much to you yet, is there? You weigh less than my jointer plane."

Molly yawned and stretched her arms wide. "He is small, isn't he?"

"I'm sorry we woke you. I was trying to be quiet so you could get some more sleep. After all you went through, I'm sure you need it. At least you got several hours. Seems we've got a good baby. He slept through the night."

She giggled. "I don't like ruining your image of parenthood, but I was up for two feedings."

"Really? I didn't hear a thing."

"You were tired."

The baby let loose with a rousing cry.

"Um, I think he needs you."

She held out her arms. "Come to Mama, my precious."

As eager as he was to get to know their son, Cole didn't mind handing the unhappy lad to Molly. "While you're taking care of him, I have an errand to run."

"On Christmas morning?"

"Mr. Stone let it slip that he'll be spending the day alone. I can't let him do that, not when we have plenty to share."

"Cole Foster, you amaze me. First Bernice and Ambrose, and now Mr. Stone? Are you feeling all right?"

He didn't know how he felt. She'd upended his entire world last night. There he'd been, looking at his son for the very first time, when she'd told him the shocking news about his father. He couldn't deny the facts. The deed clearly showed that Robert Foster had purchased the plot of land Uncle Ralph had told Cole about.

If only things had turned out differently and his pa had sent for them. Molly said he'd planned to. But if that was true, why hadn't Uncle Ralph said something before now?

HOURS LATER COLE SURVEYED THE FEAST ON the kitchen table. With Bernice's help, the picnic luncheon had turned out well. Now to surprise Molly.

She looked up when he entered the bedroom, her face aglow. Motherhood agreed with her. "That's fried chicken I smell, isn't it?"

"Sure is. You wanted a taste of summer, so you're getting one." He leaned over to take the baby from her. "Come to Papa, Bobby."

"You used the name. Does that mean...?"

"What it means is that I've been thinking. I want to forgive my pa, but I'm not ready just yet. I need to talk to Uncle Ralph first, pray, and see how things go. And I need you to be patient. Will you do that?"

She beamed. "Gladly."

He held Bobby in one arm and offered the other to Molly. "Are you sure you're up to sitting at the table?"

"Very much so. I've spent more than enough time in this room."

Molly's reaction to the meal exceeded Cole's expectations.

"And lemonade too?" She swirled the tart beverage in her glass. "How did you manage that?"

Mr. Stone plopped a second serving of potato salad on his plate. "With help from a friend." He told her what had taken place the day the lemons arrived.

Molly shifted her attention to Cole. "You still don't know who talked to Mr. Thompson?"

He smiled. "I have a hunch, but Bernice denies doing the deed."

"I didn't talk to him. Honest. But I know who did." She tilted her head toward her husband.

Cole hadn't considered the miner as his secret benefactor. "Ambrose? You did it?"

The ruddy fellow scowled at his wife, but his playful smile undermined his effort to look irritated. "Fine. It was me, but this here woman of mine was supposed to keep that to herself."

Bernice patted her husband's shoulder. "I couldn't help myself. You're a kind, generous soul, and I like folks to know that."

Cole smiled. "Thank you, Ambrose. Your gift means more than you know."

A red flush crept up the miner's neck, and he took a sudden interest in the baby girl in his lap.

Mr. Stone shoveled in his last bite of potato salad and tossed his napkin on the table. "I appreciate you sharing your Christmas dinner with me. I've had a right fine time, but you all must be plumb tuckered out after your late night. I'll be moseying on, but please accept my congratulations on your little one." He cast a glance at Bobby, who was cradled in Cole's arms.

Cole made to stand, but Mr. Stone waved him off. "I know the way out. Thanks again."

Ambrose and Bernice left soon after, leaving Cole alone with his wide-eyed son and weary wife.

Molly yawned and slapped a hand over her mouth. "I'm sorry. I'll clear things up, but then I need to lie down for a bit."

"Oh no, you don't. Bobby and I will see to that, won't we, little fellow?" He twirled a fingertip in his son's dimple.

"Then I'll accept your kind offer and take a nap." She headed for their room.

"Molly."

She paused in the doorway. "Yes?"

"Thank you for making this the best Christmas ever. I've been given a great gift today. Three, actually— our son, new friends, and an opportunity to start afresh come spring."

"Are you saying what I think you're saying?"

"I'd be a fool to turn down a prime piece of farmland."

He would work hard and make the most of the amazing gift his father had given him.

Molly crossed the room and kissed him on the cheek. "I'm glad to hear it."

Cole smiled, and Bobby wriggled in his arms.

Yes, definitely the best Christmas ever.

ABOUT THE AUTHORS

DEBBIE LYNNE COSTELLO ("The Letter") has raised four children and is now following her lifelong dream of writing. She and her husband live in upstate South Carolina with their dogs, cat, Arabian horses, and miniature donkey.

SUSAN PAGE DAVIS ("Special Delivery") has authored more than fifty books, including volumes in the Guideposts series Secrets of the Blue Hill Library, Secrets of Mary's Bookshop, Miracles of Marble Cove, and Patchwork Mysteries. She is a winner of the Carol Award, the Inspirational Readers' Choice Award, and the Will Rogers Medallion. A Maine native, Susan now lives in western Kentucky with her husband, Jim. They are the parents of six and the grandparents of nine.

KELI GWYN ("A Father's Gift"), a native Californian living in a Gold Rush-era town in the Sierra Foothills, transports readers to the early days of the Golden State. Visit her Victorian-style cyber home at KeliGwyn.com.

PAM HANSON & BARBARA ANDREWS ("Finding Something Precious") are a daughter-mother team who have written more than forty-five books in partnership, including Tales from Grace Chapel Inn, Secrets of the Blue Hill Library, and Chesapeake Antiques Mysteries for Guideposts.

MONA HODGSON ("The Family Quilt") has written nearly forty books, including the Sinclair Sisters of Cripple Creek series and six I Can Read books. Mona lives in Arizona with her husband, Bob. Learn more at MonaHodgson.com.

LIZ JOHNSON ("The Christmas Scarf") is the author of seven novels and a handful of short stories. An Arizona native, she moved to Nashville, Tennessee, four years ago and enjoys exploring Music City at Christmas and all year long. Visit her at LizJohnsonBooks.com or Facebook.com/LizJohnsonBooks.

KAE NOYCE TIENSTRA ("The Plum Pudding Phenomenon") is a book publicist and literary agent. Her articles have appeared in *Mother Earth News, Organic Gardening,* and other publications. Actress Conchata Farrell read Kae's essay "The Green

Cardigan" in a 2012 Mother's Day performance of Nora Ephron's Broadway play *Love, Loss & What I Wore.*

JACQUELINE WHEELOCK ("A Bracelet for Christmas") is an author whose works include "Christmas Lights" in *Christmas Stories from Mississippi* and her memoirs in *Children of the Changing South: Accounts of Growing Up During and After Integration.* Her first novel, *A Most Precious Gift,* debuted in September 2014. She and her husband, Donald, reside in central Mississippi.

A NOTE FROM THE EDITORS

We hope you enjoy *A Cup of Christmas Cheer*, created by the Books and Inspirational Media Division of Guideposts, a non-profit organization that touches millions of lives every day through products and services that inspire, encourage, help you grow in your faith, and celebrate God's love in every aspect of your daily life.

Thank you for making a difference with your purchase of this book, which helps fund our many outreach programs to military personnel, prisons, hospitals, nursing homes, and educational institutions. To learn more, visit GuidepostsFoundation.org.

We also maintain many useful and uplifting online resources. Visit Guideposts.org to read true stories of hope and inspiration, access OurPrayer network, sign up for free newsletters, download free e-books, join our Facebook community, and follow our stimulating blogs.

To learn about other Guideposts publications, including the best-selling devotional *Daily Guideposts*, go to ShopGuideposts.org, call (800) 932-2145, or write to Guideposts, PO Box 5815, Harlan, Iowa 51593.